W9-AEJ-565

"Did that man in your commercial turn you on?" Luke asked fiercely. *"The one you were making eyes at."*

"He's just a friend," Sassy replied lightly. "Now, how do I gather these eggs?"

"Just look at those hens the way you did your friend, and they'll do anything you want."

"What would you do if I looked at you like that?" she teased, her voice a husky whisper.

It was a question he'd been considering since the moment she arrived. Her invitation nudged him past the breaking point. Without warning, he lifted her off the ground and into the saddle, facing him.

"What—what are you doing?" she stammered, clutching his shoulders.

"Giving you the answer to your question. You did expect one, didn't you?"

She shook her head. "No, I—"

He didn't give her time to finish, but jerked her to him, smothering her protest with a savage kiss that lit fires throughout her stunned body. . . .

WHAT ARE *LOVESWEPT* ROMANCES?

They are stories of true romance and touching emotion. We believe those two very important ingredients are constants in our highly sensual and very believable stories in the *LOVESWEPT* line. Our goal is to give you, the reader, stories of consistently high quality that may sometimes make you laugh, sometimes make you cry, but are always fresh and creative and contain many delightful surprises within their pages.

Most romance fans read an enormous number of books. Those they truly love, they keep. Others may be traded with friends and soon forgotten. We hope that each *LOVESWEPT* romance will be a treasure—a "keeper." We will always try to publish

LOVE STORIES YOU'LL NEVER FORGET
BY AUTHORS YOU'LL ALWAYS REMEMBER

The Editors

LOVESWEPT® • 349

Doris Parmett
Sassy

BANTAM BOOKS
NEW YORK • TORONTO • LONDON • SYDNEY • AUCKLAND

SASSY

A Bantam Book / September 1989

LOVESWEPT® and the wave device are registered
trademarks of Bantam Books, a division of
Bantam Doubleday Dell Publishing Group, Inc.
Registered in U.S. Patent
and Trademark Office and elsewhere.

All rights reserved.
Copyright © 1989 by Doris Parmett.
Cover art copyright © 1989 by Lino Saffioti.
No part of this book may be reproduced or transmitted
in any form or by any means, electronic or mechanical,
including photocopying, recording, or by any information
storage and retrieval system, without permission in
writing from the publisher.
For information address: Bantam Books.

If you would be interested in receiving protective vinyl
covers for your Loveswept books, please write to this address
for information:

Loveswept
Bantam Books
P.O. Box 985
Hicksville, NY 11802

ISBN 0-553-22025-X

Published simultaneously in the United States and Canada

Bantam Books are published by Bantam Books, a division
of Bantam Doubleday Dell Publishing Group, Inc. Its trademark, consisting of the words "Bantam Books" and the
portrayal of a rooster, is Registered in U.S. Patent and
Trademark Office and in other countries. Marca Registrada.
Bantam Books, 666 Fifth Avenue, New York, New York 10103.

PRINTED IN THE UNITED STATES OF AMERICA

O   0 9 8 7 6 5 4 3 2 1

For Ruth and Al Pressman, my real life cowboy pals. I'm so glad you owned a ranch in Winnemucca.

Walter Kasman, a.k.a. "Y" cowboy. Your door was always open.

And to Cecilia E. Mogus, Deputy City Clerk of Winnemucca, Nevada. Special thanks for all your help.

One

Dr. Peter Reimer leaned forward, twiddled his thumbs, and dropped his bombshell. "I insist you take a vacation."

Sassy jerked upright, gripping the edge of the doctor's desk. "Peter, that's blackmail."

"I know it is," he agreed, his gray eyes twinkling. He closed the medical chart of his most famous patient, scrutinizing the beautiful blonde he'd known since she was an impish tot of two. At twenty-three Sassy had matured into an alluring young woman. Her expressive turquoise eyes were set in an oval-shaped face graced by high cheekbones. She possessed a rare beauty that the camera adored.

"Nevertheless, Sassy, you're going on vacation. Don't you realize that you fainted while filming a commercial for Lady Exquisite cosmetics? If you don't take a break, I won't authorize your insurance coverage and allow you to finish the shoot."

She shook her head. "I can't go, Pete, I wish I

could, but it's out of the question. Mother signed me to do Jamie Rudolpho's new sports layout next, and after that a movie."

Pete thumbed through an address book, finding the name he wanted. He picked up his pen. "Sassy, you don't have any options. Get away from New York, breathe fresh air, live a little. Look at something besides concrete and cameras. You're not happy. I know it, and you know it."

Sassy twisted the strap on her purse. Was she so easy to read? "Of course I'm happy. Mother is thrilled with how my career is going."

"Sassy," he said in a no-nonsense tone. "I've watched you grow up. I treated you for stomach cramps when your father and mother broke up when you were seven years old."

Tears welled up in her eyes, tears for the father who'd left because of her. "I'm the breadwinner," Sassy whispered.

"Baloney. Your mother's a highly talented woman. I know you love her, that you feel disloyal and uncomfortable right now, but someone has to tell you the truth. There are other models she can represent besides you. Honey," Peter continued in a kindly vein, "I like your mother. I really do. But you're the one who's about to make a movie. How do you feel about it?"

Sassy's lip quivered. Pete was her friend, her father confessor. "Oh, Pete, I wish I could chuck the whole thing and design clothes. That's what I really want to do, and I'm good at it."

"Then do it," he urged. "That's probably the healthiest thing you've admitted to yourself in months."

Glancing uncertainly at him, Sassy said, "Are you telling me I willed that fainting spell to happen?"

"It's a trifle more complicated, but you're not far off. Your subconscious is telling you you're ready for a change. Treadmills have a way of tripping us up. Now young lady, enough talk. If your mom gives you any guff, tell her what I said about the insurance exam. By the way, have you ever been on a ranch? It's a wonderful place to get in tune with yourself."

With the pressure off her shoulders, Sassy relaxed. She'd always dreamed of going to a dude ranch. Her friend Beth, also a high-priced model, once had regaled her with stories about the handsome men who seemed to flock to dude ranches. "I'm told a dude ranch vacation is quite an experience," she said to Pete.

Sassy imagined herself sleeping late, lazing by the pool, sipping cool drinks, eating gobs of forbidden calorie-laden foods. At night she'd dance under the stars in the arms of a strong, silent cowboy.

Peter interrupted her dreamlike reveries. He scribbled a name on a piece of paper and handed it to her. "A friend of mine, Luke Cassidy, owns a ranch not far from Winnemucca, Nevada. I'll call him and make the arrangements."

Luke Cassidy. His name had a western ring to it. Sassy let her mind drift. She wondered if he looked like Redford or Newman.

Peter recapped his pen. "I guarantee you, it will be an experience you'll never forget."

"What's Luke Cassidy's ranch like?" she asked, anxious to know more about what activities he provided for his guests.

Peter led her to the door. He signaled for his next patient. Knowing Luke the way he did, he wasn't about to be pinned down. Too bad he couldn't be a fly on the wall when those two met, he thought. "Honey, I'd love to talk, but my next patient is really ill. Have a great time." He chuckled inwardly as he closed the door.

Phyllis Shaw, a small, blond, dynamic package of a woman, paced her daughter's bedroom. Waving a manicured hand toward the open suitcases on the four-poster bed, she said, "Serena, I'll grant you that you need a vacation, and I probably can stall Rudolpho, but why the Cassidy ranch? It's not on anybody's list. At least go to Palm Springs. I'll phone my publicity contacts there."

Sassy folded a blouse. She snapped the locks on her suitcases, then put on her brightest smile. "Mother, wish me a good time."

Phyllis pouted. "If you insist on going, leave me the phone number of the godforsaken place and stay out of the sun. An uneven tan is the kiss of death for a model. And don't eat too much. Those places are notorious for their fattening barbecues and rich desserts. Remember, the camera adds weight."

Sassy laughed. Nothing ever changed. "Thanks, darling. Now stand up, kiss me good-bye, and tell me you're delighted I'm going."

"I'm delighted you're going," her mother said in an unconvincing tone, then good-naturedly kissed her daughter good-bye.

"Well, hell," Luke Cassidy muttered, pushing the wheat-colored Stetson back on his head. He thought of all the reasons he had not to be at the airport. He belonged at the ranch. But Pete had all but twisted his arm, talking a mile a minute until he'd given in just to shut him up so he could go back to the hundred things that needed his attention.

Mentally he began to list them. Coyotes were killing some of his calves. It hadn't rained in weeks. The windrower had broken down leaving the alfalfa half cut in the fields, and he needed it for winter feed. The lousy baler had broken down too. Nothing could get done until the equipment was fixed.

On top of that horrendous mess, his men were upset because Maria, the best cook west of the Mississippi, had left in a hurry to take care of her sister who'd given birth prematurely.

And as if all that weren't bad enough, the stupid commuter plane from Reno was late. Instead of cooling his heels waiting for some fancy stuck-up model, what he should be doing was finding a cook. Fast. Hardworking men needed to know where their next meal was coming from. One of these days his good nature would be his undoing, he realized. There just weren't enough hours in the day. He'd even complained to Pete about his run of bad luck when they'd spoken.

"Maybe Sassy'll change it," Pete had stated.

Luke doubted it.

"How come she's not going to a spa or a fancy dude ranch?" Luke had asked Pete. "She's bound to be bored stiff. I've got better things to do than play nursemaid to a city girl."

"Give her a chance, Luke," Pete had argued cheerily. "We both know going to a dude ranch is like play acting. Let her help out around the place. All she needs is a little fresh air and a nice quiet place to sort out some decisions she has to make. I happen to think it's important for her to live like a normal person for a while. She's due to start a movie soon. You know what that's like."

Luke did know, and he never wanted to look back. He'd lived on the edge for too many years. Working as a professional stuntman had almost killed him. A firing mechanism had gone haywire on the set one day and had blown up close to him. He'd been hospitalized for months.

But it had also been his lucky day, because Pete happened to have been visiting the set with a friend. His fast action had literally saved Luke's life—and his leg. But the accident had ended Luke's career. While he'd been laid up, he'd had plenty of time to think about his life. He'd decided finally to spend his savings and put to use the degree in animal husbandry and ranch management he'd gotten before going into the hazardous profession of stunt work.

The accident had also helped to open his eyes to

the true nature of women. At the time, he'd been engaged to a starlet who'd had high ambitions. He'd dismissed the fact that Cynthia rarely had come to the hospital and had convinced himself that he wanted to concentrate on his rehabilitation.

After he'd bought the ranch, Cynthia had visited him there. Once. She'd seen desolation where he saw nature's wonders. "I'll be buried out here, Luke. I've got to think of my career."

Shifting to a more comfortable position, he propped his booted foot against the concrete wall of the airport building. What was it Pete had said? "Don't treat Sassy as if she's special. Let her help out. Find something for her to do."

She'll do the cooking, Luke decided, pleased by his inspiration borne of desperation. He could get his men to put up with a lot of things, but he couldn't expect ten hardworking ranch hands to miss their meals.

Sassy peered out of the airplane window, awed by the sight of the Humboldt mountain range. The mountains resembled majestic purple capes. Far below, winding like a giant blue snake, the Humboldt River wended its way along the desert floor. Excitement rippled through her. She couldn't believe she was actually starting her vacation. She was as free as a bird for the first time in ages. Her friend Beth's parting words came back to her. "Set your sights on the best-looking man, Sassy. And take plenty of sexy clothes. Don't spend your whole time sketching designs."

With her luggage claim tickets safely tucked in her pocket, Sassy stood at the top of the ramp, her eyes searching, hoping Luke Cassidy had remembered to send a limousine to pick her up.

As she descended the flight of steps and headed for the terminal, she saw a tall cowboy angle away from the wall. A wide leather belt rode low on his hips. She was momentarily blinded by the rays of the sun bouncing off the hammered gold belt buckle. Her pulse speeded up as he came nearer and she got a better look at him.

The man's walk was slow and easy and suggestive. He sauntered closer with the kind of gait that could make a woman pant. She knew many a male model who practiced for hours in front of a mirror to accomplish what this blatantly masculine man seemed to do naturally.

He was long and lean with broad shoulders. He wore mud-spattered boots, faded jeans, and a blue cotton shirt with the sleeves rolled up, which displayed biceps that looked like burnished steel. He dripped with rugged male confidence.

By anyone's standards, this good-looking cowboy was a fantasy come true. If the rest of the cowboys at the ranch were anything like this one, Sassy thought, her vacation was off to a flying start.

Unconsciously, she touched her upper lip with the tip of her tongue. *Bless you for ordering me to take a rest, Peter Reimer,* she said silently. *I'm going to enjoy myself!*

As if she'd willed it, the cowboy whipped off his sunglasses, allowing her to see his eyes.

Mmmm. *Nice eyes,* she thought. Just a hint of danger in their depths. They were midnight black, the same shade as his hair, which in true cowboy fashion was too long. A mustache, full and slightly drooping at the sides, curved over a finely sculpted mouth. His face was tanned and taut.

He wasn't Redford or Newman. He was handsomer. Luke felt as if he were being dissected. He also felt something he hadn't felt in a long time—a definite attraction to a woman. What the hell, he thought. He had the time. Her luggage wasn't off the plane yet. She'd sized him up, so he returned the compliment.

She sure was pretty. Her face was framed by a lush wild mane of blond hair that glistened in the sun. Her skin was flawless, which didn't surprise him. He knew models kept themselves in perfect condition.

His prurient gaze skimmed over her long shapely legs. He could almost imagine his hands on her silky skin teasing the hem of her short skirt. He'd always been a sucker for a woman in a mini skirt.

Her ankle-length boots would be as impractical on the ranch as the patterned red stockings she wore to match her bright red blouse, he noticed. But, oh, what a glorious sight!

He let his gaze skim slowly upward, taking in the flush on her cheeks. It pleased him to think he'd put it there. He wished she'd take her sunglasses off so he could see her eyes. They were hidden behind saucer-size frames. Hers was a face that demanded leisurely exploration, he decided. Peter hadn't been wrong when he'd called her a knockout.

Beautiful but spoiled, Luke thought, reminding himself he had been burned before by a pampered self-indulgent actress.

He thrust out his hand as she approached him. "You must be Sassy. If you'll give me your claim tickets, I'll gather up your luggage and we'll get going."

She shook his hand and gave him a warm hello, then dropped the ticket stubs into his palm. Counting them, he shot her a glance of disbelief. "Do you always travel with five suitcases?" Recounting the tickets, he muttered "Women," then turned on his heel.

Sassy wasn't used to being dismissed. "Just a minute," she said. "Do you have a problem with women?"

His brows lifted, and he took a long look at her. A half-smile played at his lips. Shaking his head, he strode off in the direction of the baggage area.

Sassy struggled to keep up with his long strides. Grudgingly, she admitted he looked as good from the rear as he did from the front. If you liked nice tight buns, she thought.

Inside the terminal Luke sat down on one of the hard molded chairs, crossed his legs at the ankle, and then tapped his foot impatiently. As soon as the luggage was brought in, he surged forward to find Sassy's.

Sassy had to agree that she may have gone overboard with her luggage, but she never claimed to be an efficient packer. She envied flight attendants who were able to put everything they needed in a case the size of a lunch box. She supposed it was because she never had to worry about how much she brought with her on a location shoot. Someone was always around to handle her bags.

"Come on."

"Where's the car?" Sassy asked. The cowboy hefted her suitcases under his arms as if they were filled with feathers. Angling his head, he motioned for her to follow him outside.

"There it is."

Sassy sucked in a blast of hot desert air and blinked. The monstrosity parked at the curb was the scrungiest excuse for a pickup truck she'd ever seen in her life. Attached to the rear was a horse trailer. Inside it, their long tails swishing at flies, were two noisy horses.

Sassy gnashed her teeth and balled her fists as the cowboy nonchalantly tossed her matched set of Gucci luggage onto a pile of feed in the back of the pickup.

"Don't mind them," the cowboy said, referring to the noisy animals. "They're hungry. Hop in."

Sassy knew she was in trouble.

Mini skirts worked beautifully when riding in limousines, moderately well in vans, but were out of the question if one was expected to hop into the front seat of a pickup. Behind her she heard the cowboy mutter about all the things he still had to do. She nearly jumped out of her skin when she felt his warm breath on her neck. In a flash he lifted her up, dumping her on the torn brown vinyl bench seat. "Can't waste all day."

No wonder her mother had never heard of the Cassidy Dude Ranch. Peter obviously hadn't been there in a while, or maybe he knew his friend faced bankruptcy and wanted to help, Sassy thought as she swept her gaze over the interior of the truck. The floor was littered with candy wrappers. Gum wrappers overflowed from the cigarette tray. Luke seemed to read her mind. "Better than smoking. Buckle up." He gunned the engine and they took off.

Sassy didn't know what to make of him. When he touched her, she could swear lightning had struck in broad daylight. She'd heard that cowboys were mostly silent, but this official greeter carried it too far. He hadn't even told her his name, and she wasn't about to give him the satisfaction of asking.

Hired help, she knew, was hard to get, harder still to keep, so she'd said nothing when he grumbled about being late for his errands, complained about her luggage, plopped her in the seat, and ordered her to buckle up. Hiding behind her huge dark sunglasses, she contemplated him in private.

Tom Selleck he isn't! she thought.

"Tell me about the town," she asked.

Luke glanced at her, as if deciding whether it was worth his trouble to give the usual tourist speech.

"Winnemucca's pretty small by your standards.

We don't have millions of people or skyscrapers to blot out the sun. The population is about six thousand, but if you add in the ranchers and the farmers, it's eleven thousand, more or less."

What did he know about her standards? "I read that the Pony Express used to come through."

"Yup," he answered laconically. Sassy was all set to defend her existence, to show him she'd come prepared for her western trek, then she saw that he didn't seem in the least bit interested. Having given his opinion on life in the Big Apple, he kept his eyes on the road.

Sassy had conveniently forgotten that one of her fantasies had been to find a cowboy who spoke in the abbreviated way of Gary Cooper. But the fact that he wasn't talking didn't mean she couldn't take in the view. She studied his profile, comparing him to some of the men she knew.

She had grown up in a business where one's face, one's walk, the way one looked into the camera's all-knowing lens meant success or failure. She viewed the man next to her with a critical eye.

There was a rugged strength in his face, from the chiseled forehead to the straight nose, to his square jaw. His hands on the wheel reflected the same quiet determination she saw in his rugged countenance. She couldn't imagine him modeling.

His mustache lifted, and she thought she'd caught a hint of a smile, but it disappeared so quickly, she couldn't be sure. "Well, do I pass?" he asked in a rich baritone voice.

She lifted her chin a notch. On a scale of one to ten, he annoyed her a twelve. "Depends on what the test is." The last thing she expected was to hear him chuckle.

Feeling as though she'd been caught with her hand in the cookie jar, she turned her head to stare out at the desert countryside. She'd save her questions for Luke Cassidy.

In the meantime she settled back to enjoy the beauty of the desert colors, thinking how she'd use them in a collection of her designs. Her mind raced as she tried to file away the malachite greens, mineral grays, Prussian blues, burnt siennas, brilliant yellows, and soft tans. Suddenly the car took a bump, as the cowboy swerved around rolling tumbleweeds that were skittering across the highway. He didn't say anything until they pulled into the parking lot of a supermarket. "Wait a minute," he said when she reached for the door handle. "I'll give you a hand." He slid off the seat and came around to her side.

For the second time she felt his strong hands on her waist. Her heart fluttered. There was no denying his potent masculinity. His arms were corded with muscles. The cotton shirt, opened at the neck, allowed her a glimpse of dark chest hair. He smelled of the outdoors and leather, a heady mixture.

For a moment he didn't move but quietly looked down at her from his superior height. She caught her breath and lowered her eyes. Easy, Sassy, she told herself, don't make more of this than there is. He was only preventing her from breaking a leg and suing his boss.

Luke tossed his hat into the cab. He glanced at her questioningly. "Do you mind helping me shop? We need some provisions for the ranch. Maria, our cook, had to leave in a hurry. Her sister's baby came early."

It was the first almost friendly speech he'd made to her. There was something irresistible about a cowboy with a mustache and dimples. Besides, she decided, she wanted to find out more about his boss.

Hoping to draw him into conversation, she said, "I would think a dude ranch employed more than one chef."

Her statement clearly surprised him. He put his hand on her arm. "Just a minute. Did Peter tell you my ranch was a dude ranch?"

She whipped off her glasses, barely hearing his intake of breath as he saw her eyes for the first time. She jerked her head upward.

"You're Luke Cassidy." It sounded like an accusation.

An eyebrow flicked upward. "Who did you think I was?" he asked, leaning toward her. Her eyes were an extraordinary shade of blue-green.

"How was I supposed to know? You were too busy being rude. Where I come from people exchange names. What kind of a ranch do you own?" she asked, not caring if her tone was less than polite.

The muscles in his jaw tensed. He'd come perilously close to enjoying himself when he'd lifted her out of the pickup. She was soft and womanly, scented with wildflowers. For a moment he'd even forgiven Peter for shipping her to him.

"What kind of ranch?" she demanded.

He shoved his hands in his pockets. "A cow and calf ranch."

Her chin dropped. She understood for the first time why he thought her nuts for traveling with so many suitcases. Steaming mad, both at herself and at Peter, she wheeled around abruptly, disregarding the stares of curious onlookers, many of whom greeted Luke. To them he was friendly!

Her dream vacation, the vacation her mother had tried to get her to cancel, the vacation Peter had assured her would be a vacation of a lifetime, had turned out to be a disaster. She'd come all the way from New York to see nothing more exciting than a bunch of cows! She wanted to scream.

"Not a dude ranch," she said through clenched teeth. "No chuck wagon parties. No dances. No hayrides. No swimming pool. None of that. Just cows and calves."

"And chickens," Luke supplied, getting the general idea of what was going through her mind. He put his hand over his mouth to hide his laughter.

Disgusted, she threw up her hands and glared at him.

Pulling a straight face he said, "The Basque Festival was in June. Too bad you missed it. Besides a big parade, Basque dancing, wood chopping, weight lifting, and a demonstration by working sheep dogs, we marinate lamb in spices, then have a big barbecue. There's sourdough bread, salsa, and pie. Then again," he said, working hard to maintain a serious look, "if it's a little romance you're looking for, you can always watch the bulls mate with the cows. The last time I looked, they weren't shy."

"Very funny!" she said.

Luke's mirth spilled out. His eyes met hers, and he shook with laughter until it was all out of his system. He put his hands on her shoulders, creating another kind of tension in her. "Come on," he urged. "Ease up."

Sassy began to see the ridiculousness of the situation. It didn't, however, make her less furious with him, mostly because he was triggering all kinds of unwanted responses along her nerve endings.

Luke attempted to make peace. "Look, we might as well make the best of a bad situation. Pete said you needed to get away to a place off the beaten path for a while. You're welcome to stay at the ranch as long as you want, if you think you can take it." His tone clearly intimated he thought otherwise.

Sassy pushed his hands away. She didn't know whether to laugh or cry. She was too wrung out to ask what Luke meant by "take it" or how much money "take it" was going to cost her.

Peter wasn't at fault, she realized. Thinking back, he'd never really gone into detail. After listening to Beth rave about the pleasures of a dude ranch vacation, she foolishly assumed Luke's ranch was a dude ranch too. Her romantic notions had carried her along.

She'd also packed enough clothes to choke a horse—funky off-the-shoulder tops, cropped shorts, a beaded cocktail dress, and Beth's present to her, a daring bathing suit that had made her blush when she'd first seen it. The suit consisted of a series of black strings that covered the bare essentials.

She'd stepped out of the plane wearing a drop-dead mini skirt, and all the time Tom Selleck alias Luke Cassidy owned a cow and calf ranch in the middle of the desert!

What made Peter think Luke Cassidy and his ranch were a sure cure for what ailed her?

"Naturally," Luke drawled, shifting his weight, "I'd expect you to do your share."

She didn't trust the sly look on his face. "Meaning?"

He grinned. "You'll cook breakfast tomorrow morning." He hooked his thumbs in his belt, waiting for her answer.

Everything about his stance said he thought she'd be on the next plane out. Well, she wasn't about to give him the satisfaction. Besides, her mother had the phone number of the ranch. Leaving now would be tantamount to admitting failure.

Sassy was no slouch in the kitchen. Cooking relaxed her. She faithfully treated herself to one decent breakfast a week. Every Sunday morning she ate one piece of whole wheat toast with diet margarine and apricot jam spread on it, a poached egg, cranberry juice, and black coffee. The other mornings her normal fare consisted of two tablespoons of low-calorie cottage cheese with a tablespoon of bran sprinkled on top, and a glass of orange juice.

If scrambling a couple of eggs and frying a few slices of bacon would keep Luke from telling Peter what a fool she'd made of herself, she'd fix his meal.

"I'll make breakfast tomorrow morning," she said sweetly. She'd also gladly cram it down his hand-some throat.

Two

Shopping with Luke was an experience.

In her mind he ranked as the all-time original impulse buyer. As soon as he filled one cart, he wheeled it to the front, left it there, then charged down the aisle to begin the process again with another cart. Occasionally he'd catch her gaping at him. He'd raise his eyebrows momentarily, then return with renewed gusto to his foraging.

After three wagons joined the first, Sassy couldn't stand it. "How often do you shop?"

He answered without breaking stride. "Maria usually does all the shopping, but she didn't leave a list. I'm only getting a few things to tide us over. Mind getting me four of those, please."

"Those" were four sacks of flour. While she bent down to the lower shelf, he reached over her head for two boxes of rice. They came to the meat counter next, and there Sassy was convinced he'd had a

SASSY • 21

deprived childhood or else he had no sense when it came to budgeting.

Into the cart went five sugar-cured hams, four standing rib roasts, twenty-five steaks, seven tur-keys, and eight packages of chicken. He thought a moment, then casually tossed in ten more steaks.

He grinned. "We usually butcher our own, but with the equipment breakdown, there's no time."

Sassy watched in morbid fascination. Both she and her mother counted calories and judged the nutritional value of the food that went into their bodies. Not so, apparently, Luke. She wondered if the pickup truck would hold all the food or whether they'd have to press the horse trailer into service.

"Are you sure you bought enough?" she asked, smiling, when they went to the checkout counter.

He paused in the act of tearing off the wrapper of a bar of chocolate. He motioned to the cashier to charge him for it. He cocked an eye at her. "What's your real name?"

She counted the other bars he'd put on the counter. "Serena."

He grinned and shook his head. "Sassy suits you better."

"Anybody ever tell you chocolate's bad for the skin?"

"Is that all you models think about?" he asked as he polished off the candy bar and licked his lips.

"I wish it were," Sassy answered under her breath.

Outside, Luke helped her into the cab again. And once more she experienced a surge of pleasure from the simple gesture. She was no longer peeved by the idea of not going to a dude ranch. She'd be able to experience the real McCoy rather than a contrived sense of what ranching was all about.

"Is your place far from here?" she asked after they'd been traveling on the interstate for fifteen minutes.

"Not far. About eighteen miles." He was trying to be polite and friendly, but something, she knew, was bugging him. From the moment he'd put his arms around her and lifted her into the truck, his face had settled into a grim mask. It was hard to figure him out. One minute he gave her the impression he didn't resent her company, and the next he reverted to stony silence.

"I'd like to know about your ranch, Luke."

He gazed at her for what seemed an eternity. "It's 48,000 acres. But the bureau of Land Management allows the ranchers to use 350,000 acres of state-owned property. The land's pretty arid out here, so we need large tracts for the cows to graze and find water."

There was open space as far as her eye could see. "It's lovely country though."

"Not everyone would agree with you."

She heard a trace of bitterness in his tone, but didn't want to question him about it. "If everyone mixes up the herds, how do you know which animals belong to you?"

"During the year the men ride the range, keeping an eye on things. Our cows are already branded, and a calf won't leave its mother. The ranch hands notch the calves' ears. "This way we can identify ours. We cull the herds in the roundup, brand the calves, and take the cattle to auction."

Fascinated, she asked, "What if they miss one?"

He shrugged his shoulder. "Our tough luck. It's known as a slick calf. Anyone may claim it."

"You make it sound so easy." The enormity of the logistics dazzled her.

"It's hard work," he said with a tolerant glance. "Especially during the roundup. All the families pitch in, helping in whatever way they can."

Her interest piqued, she asked, "When is that? I'd like to go."

His gaze swept over her, taking in her mini skirt, her stockinged legs, her long manicured fingernails, her perfect makeup. He remembered how soft she felt in his arms, the scent of her perfume. "In the first place, it's next month. In the second place, it's not for you," he said with finality.

"Why?" she asked, annoyed at being considered a hothouse flower. "Did you ever think that if I were here, I could help out the women in some way? You said yourself, everyone goes."

He pushed his foot down on the pedal, then eased up when the horses began making a racket. "I know exactly what I said. I said everyone pitches in. That assumes the people involved know what they're doing and won't get in the way."

She opened her mouth to protest, but Luke continued. "Don't go getting a lot of foolish ideas about roundups. They're anything but romantic—stinking horse flesh, sweating cows, and choking dust. Life on a ranch is rigorous. The hours are long and hard. Any number of things can and do go wrong. A man never knows if he'll get home for dinner or spend the night with a sick animal."

Speech or no speech, Sassy was not about to back off. "Does Maria go?"

"Maria's in charge of the Circle C chuck wagon. Look, if you want to play roundup, Sassy, check into a dude ranch that features it as entertainment. My insurance doesn't cover you."

She decided to give up. Not because of his impolite rebuke. There was no doubt that he was right. She gave up simply because it wasn't worth the effort to argue. She was a guest, albeit an uninvited one. Peter had probably twisted his arm to get him to accept her.

Not one of Peter's better ideas, she realized. Luke, whatever she might think of his mercurial moods, owned his ranch, and he certainly had a right to expect it to function without unnecessary complications from her.

Just the same, she mused, focusing on another idea, she intended to learn to ride a horse without falling off, even if she had to learn behind Luke's back.

Sassy watched him covertly, knew she'd irritated him. Attempting to smooth things over, she asked, "When will we be on your land?"

"We've been riding on it for the last five miles. The house is about a mile down the road."

Sassy rubbed her eyes, sat up straighter, and stared out at the passing scenery.

Luke pointed to a nearby creek. His gaze traveled

over her face. She was not a woman to take lightly. She could make a man want. Once he'd been burned. Once, but never again.

"Believe it or not," he said, reverting to his role as host, "that creek widens into a river not far from here. It starts as a stream up in the mountains close to one of our line shacks. One of these days I'm going to dam up part of it, pipe in some of the mineral springs, and build a swimming pool, although there is one I use up in the hills."

She was eager to see the natural hot springs. "I'd like to swim in it as long as I'm here."

He decided that when she wasn't talking nonsense, she was an enjoyable woman to be with. Even her misplaced desire to play cowgirl hadn't really annoyed him, though he suspected she wasn't through pushing yet. She'd given in too easily. Girls like Sassy didn't get as far as she had without knowing exactly when to push. He already knew that she was obstinate.

Without thinking, he patted her thigh. " 'Fraid you'll burn that cute little tush of yours. The water's hot enough to boil eggs."

A thrill raced through Sassy. Luke Cassidy, it seemed, wasn't impervious to her charms, even if she were sitting on them. "I guess I'll have to settle for a nice hot bath instead."

His gaze lingered on her full, sensuous mouth. Touching her nylon-clad thigh had been like touching velvet. He wasn't about to make that mistake again. Once a fool . . . "Don't let Buster hear you."

"Buster?" She'd almost felt the intimate touch of Luke's gaze, and her pulse quickened.

"Mmmm. My dog. He thinks he's a canine Greg Luganis. You should see him dive. Cuts the water better than a lot of swimmers I've seen. Behave yourself, and if you like, you can swim in the natural pool I mentioned up in the hills."

She'd like that. She'd also like it if Luke joined her. She imagined how he'd look in a bathing suit, all muscled and strong. "Will you take me?"

"No. I'll have Chester show you the place, if he has the time after work. I'm too busy."

So much for her foolish romantic notions. When she thought she'd made two inches of headway, Luke infuriatingly pushed her back three. He was as slippery as a snake and, she suspected, about as dangerous.

"Chester?"

"Chester's my foreman. Here we are."

They'd reached the end of the long road. Luke's home was a rambling white ranch with a Spanish tile roof extending over a wide wood-planked porch. Pink, white, and red geraniums planted in giant clay pots added a touch of color. Off to the side of the house was a satellite communications dish. There were several other structures on the premises.

"That's the bunkhouse where the men sleep when they're not on the range," Luke explained.

Sassy nodded, searching for signs of activity. She didn't see any. "And that?"

"That's a chicken coop. The other is the stable for the horses."

IF YOU LOVE ROMANCE...
THEN YOU'RE READY TO BE "LOVESWEPT"!

Mail this heart today! (see inside)

**LOVESWEPT INVITES YOU
TO OPEN YOUR HEART
TO LOVE
AND WE'LL GIVE YOU
6 FREE BOOKS
A FREE LIGHTED MAKEUP CASE
AND MUCH MORE**

OPEN YOUR HEART TO LOVE...
YOU'LL BE LOVESWEPT WITH THIS FREE OFFER!

HERE'S WHAT YOU GET:

1. FREE! SIX NEW LOVESWEPT NOVELS! You get 6 beautiful stories filled with passion, romance, laughter, and tears... exciting romances to stir the excitement of falling in love... again and again.

2. FREE! A BEAUTIFUL MAKEUP CASE WITH A MIRROR THAT LIGHTS UP! What could be more useful than a makeup case with a mirror that lights up*? Once you open the tortoise-shell finish case, you have a choice of brushes... for your lips, your eyes, and your blushing cheeks.

*(batteries not included)

3. SAVE! MONEY-SAVING HOME DELIVERY! Join the Loveswept at-home reader service and we'll send you 6 new novels each month. You always get 15 days to preview them before you decide. Each book is yours for only $2.09 — a savings of 41¢ per book.

4. BEAT THE CROWDS! You'll always receive your Loveswept books before they are available in bookstores. You'll be the first to thrill to these exciting new stories.

BE LOVESWEPT TODAY — JUST COMPLETE, DETACH AND MAIL YOUR FREE-OFFER CARD.

FREE–LIGHTED MAKEUP CASE!
FREE–6 LOVESWEPT NOVELS!

- NO OBLIGATION
- NO PURCHASE NECESSARY

(DETACH AND MAIL CARD TODAY.)

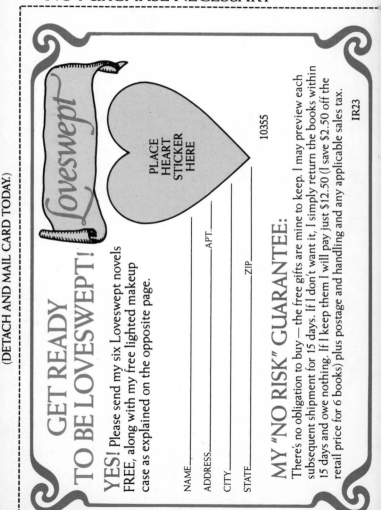

Loveswept

GET READY TO BE LOVESWEPT!

YES! Please send my six Loveswept novels FREE, along with my free lighted makeup case as explained on the opposite page.

NAME_____

ADDRESS_____APT.____

CITY_____

STATE_____ZIP_____

PLACE HEART STICKER HERE

10355

MY "NO RISK" GUARANTEE:

There's no obligation to buy — the free gifts are mine to keep. I may preview each subsequent shipment for 15 days. If I don't want it, I simply return the books within 15 days and owe nothing. If I keep them I will pay just $12.50 (I save $2.50 off the retail price for 6 books) plus postage and handling and any applicable sales tax.

IR23

REMEMBER!

- The free books and gift are mine to keep!
- There is no obligation!
- I may preview each shipment for 15 days!
- I can cancel anytime!

(DETACH AND MAIL CARD TODAY.)

NO POSTAGE
NECESSARY
IF MAILED
IN THE
UNITED STATES

BUSINESS REPLY MAIL
FIRST-CLASS MAIL   PERMIT NO. 2456   HICKSVILLE, N.Y.

POSTAGE WILL BE PAID BY ADDRESSEE

Loveswept

Bantam Books
P.O. Box 985
Hicksville, NY 11802-9827

He opened the back door of the horse trailer and led the horses into a fenced corral. Then he came around to her side and scooped her up in his arms as if he'd been doing it for years. She liked the feel of being near him and loved the way his eyelids seemed to become heavy when they were close to each other.

Just as he started to lower her to the ground, he swung her up and around. "Uh oh. Brace yourself. Buster's about to say hello."

A lop-eared mongrel the size of a Great Dane lunged off the porch and flew toward them. He crashed to a halt at Luke's feet, kicking up a flurry of dust. Sassy instinctively cringed.

"Easy," Luke said in a soothing voice as he held her tighter. "Buster only wants to get to know your scent. Don't be afraid."

She'd never been allowed to own a dog. "Would you mind *telling* him how I smell?" she asked in a shaky voice.

He felt a shiver of fear run through her. He stroked her back with his free hand. Unable to help himself, he rubbed his cheek in her thick mane of hair, catching a whiff of her elusive scent.

"Buster wouldn't harm a fly."

She eyed the dog's sharp incisors. "Buster may not plan to hurt a fly, but I don't trust the size of his teeth."

"'He's an old pussycat. Trust me." Sassy shook her head.

"Buster, heel," Luke commanded.

To her relief the dog heeled. Then Luke said, "Buster, roll over." Buster rolled over. Sassy began to relax and to enjoy the performance, especially since she felt safe in Luke's arms. Then Luke said, "Buster, play dead."

To her utter amazement, the dog emitted a woeful moan, lowered his body to the ground, rolled over, and shuddered. He lifted up all four paws, giving every impression of being dead to the world.

Luke nudged the dog's rump. "Buster, wake up and tell the lady you're sorry for scaring her." On cue Buster returned to life. He held his paws together as if in prayer.

"How does he do that?" Sassy asked, still clinging to Luke, more because it felt so wonderful than out of any lingering fear.

"Buster's a retired actor," he said, surprising her.

She turned her face to ask Luke a question. When she did, her lips brushed his cheek. His fingers tensed on her arm. For a moment their gazes locked. Neither moved. Then Luke eased her down, motioning for Buster to stay.

Sassy cautiously put her hand out to pat the dog's head. Then she stroked his shiny coat, laughing when Buster's tail wagged furiously. The more he wagged, the more she stroked. The two were acting as if they were old buddies.

Luke couldn't help beaming at the sight. "I think you've made a friend for life."

She glanced up, her eyes shining. Luke had helped her overcome her fear in a way that hadn't made her feel embarrassed. "I can see Buster must have made a terrific actor. Did you train him?"

"That's a long story," Luke said, avoiding it by

going to the truck to start unloading the bags of food. Sassy shrugged her shoulders and trotted after him. She had the feeling she'd reached a door, then had had it politely but firmly closed in her face. He convinced her of it by changing the subject.

"Tell me about the movie you're going to make." Luke said, his arms filled with bags of food.

Sassy picked up two of the lighter ones. "It's a story about a woman at the crossroads of her life. I'm not sure how it ends. The script is being revised."

The theme reminded Luke of his conversation with Peter. He made no further comment. Life and art often imitated each other. In any case her private affairs were none of his concern.

Sassy followed him up the steps to the house. He led her into a large white-tiled kitchen. Two redwood picnic tables and benches were in the center of the room. Two stoves stood side by side near a blue-and-white-tiled counter. Oversize pots and pans hung from a rack above a butcher-block chopping table, which formed an **L** to the counter.

"Come on, I'll show you the place, then I'll bring in the rest of the stuff while you unpack."

The house wasn't new nor was the furniture. It was furnished, Sassy saw quickly as they entered the living room, in a decidedly masculine style, from the deep oversize brown couches to the large wing chairs flanking the fireplace.

Sassy walked over to a bookcase that stood in a corner. She noticed the books covered a wide range of reading tastes, including animal husbandry, farm management, and surprisingly several on the subject of movie stuntmen.

Curious, Sassy reached for one of the books. Behind her she heard Luke mutter under his breath. Turning, she saw the scowl on his face and glanced down at the book in her hand.

"Luke, you wrote this," she said, amazed. "You—you were a stuntman." Her eyes glowed. "But that's wonderful."

Luke took the book from her hand and put it back on the shelf. "It was a long time ago," he said curtly. "I'm not ashamed of being a stuntman, but I prefer to forget it. Buster worked in my movies. I trained him. When I quit, he quit."

The grim set to his mouth told her to drop the subject. She put her hand on his arm. "Whatever your reasons for quitting, Luke, I'm sure they were important."

He nodded briefly, then led her into the dining room. There was a lovely round oak table with ten chairs, large enough, Sassy thought, to accommodate a big family. The sideboard was also oak. It was a charming old piece with a beveled mirror set into the top cabinet.

She wondered if Luke had ever married, but after the way he refused to discuss his former career, she didn't dare query him about his private life, instead she focused on his tour of the house.

Suspended from the ceiling was a light fixture fashioned from a wagon wheel. "Did you make it?" she asked, sensing there was nothing he couldn't do if he put his mind to it.

He shrugged his shoulders. "It's easy, really. Anybody with the right tools could."

"I couldn't, " she said truthfully, "even with the right tools."

He waited while she studied the sepia-toned pictures and framed documents hanging on the wall. One was of the original land grant. "This way I won't lose it," Luke explained.

From there they went to his study. Aerial pictures of the ranch hung on the walls. A window overlooked the mountains and the paddock. Luke's oak desk was massive, his brown leather chair well worn. On a separate table was a computer and printer.

Buster padded along by Sassy's side. From time to time she reached down to stroke his fur.

Luke opened the door to another room, then stepped aside to let her enter. "Here we are."

Sassy gasped in happy surprise. The room that was to be hers was decorated beautifully. As masculine as the other rooms were, this one spoke of quiet elegance. It was exquisite in its attention to detail. Whoever had decorated the room had lavished it with love.

Leaded bowed windows overlooked the mountains. Dominating one wall was a king-size bed with a scrolled wood-frame headboard. Lush cabbage roses overprinted in shades of dusty green-and-rose Egyptian cotton, set on a pale peach background, were repeated in the fabric of the bedspread, valance, and curtains. To soften and complement the floral design, a medley of heart-, round-, square-, and oblong-shaped, white-on-white lace-trimmed boudoir pillows was nestled against the shams.

She admired the pair of crystal candlesticks on the vanity table on the wall opposite the bed. In their holders were scented candles. Next to the candlesticks was a lace-trimmed picture frame that held no picture. She glanced up, seeing the tight expression on Luke's face. Luke, she realized with a pang of sympathy, had decorated this room for a woman, and she had hurt him very badly.

Sassy crossed over to the window. A light breeze fanned her face, lifting her hair at the sides. Turning away from the captivating sight of the mountains in the distance, she said, "This is the loveliest bedroom I've ever seen. Any woman would be lucky to have it. Imagine, tomorrow I'll not only wake up in the beauty of this room, but also I'll be able to look at the beauty of the view."

"It's just a guest room," he said brusquely. She was beautiful, he thought as he watched her, and she seemed completely at ease in the room. She was tall yet delicate, with alabaster skin. He opened a door that led to a connecting bathroom.

"Everything you need is in the linen closet. I'll be back with the rest of your things." His flat voice and blunt dismissal left her reeling. Did Peter know how much hurt this man carried with him?

Luke deposited her makeup case on the vanity table. He put another small case on the hope chest at the foot of the bed. The others he placed on the bed. "You must be hungry."

"Not really, but I would like one of the apples you

bought." He started to go, but she stopped him. "Luke."

"Yes?" His hand was on the knob.

"I want to thank you for letting me stay. I'll try to keep out of your way." She sat down on the bed, feeling like an intruder. "Don't forget to wake me to cook breakfast tomorrow."

"Are you sure? Maybe you'd prefer to sleep in?"

She lifted her hair from her neck in an unconscious gesture that held Luke's attention. "No. I'd love to have breakfast with you. Wake me when you get up. Besides, I want you to see what a good cook I am." She yawned. "If you wouldn't mind bringing the apple in, I'll unpack and take a bath."

He looked at her sitting on the bed for a long moment, then nodded and left. He returned with the apple and a glass of milk. "I thought you might be thirsty." He beckoned to the dog. "Come on, Buster. Leave the lady alone."

Buster sidled closer to Sassy and sat down on his haunches. Luke shook his head in wry amusement. "You're ruining a fine actor. At this rate he won't do a thing I say."

Sassy chuckled. She put her arm around Buster's neck. "Let him stay," she said, scratching the fur behind the dog's ear. "You have no idea how good it feels not to be afraid of him any longer. Besides, he'll keep me company. I imagine with all this quiet, it can get pretty scary here at night. I'm used to all the lights and noise of the city."

Luke hadn't thought he would be affected by seeing another woman in this room. Or maybe it was this particular woman with her natural grace and beauty. He'd be glad when her visit was over. One would-be actress in his life had been enough.

"All right, but if he bothers you, kick him out. 'Night, Sassy. If you need anything, I'll be right next door."

Her hand suddenly stilled on the dog's fur. Emotions tumbled across her face. "Next door?"

He wondered if she knew how expressive her eyes were. She'd been as transparent as glass. "Sassy, this isn't a hotel. It's a house. Peter should have explained that. My room adjoins this one. I can't put you in Maria's bedroom, and the others are used for storage."

"Luke, I didn't mean . . ."

His gaze roamed over her. "I know exactly what you meant. Forget it. Get some sleep, kid. You look beat."

Three

Luke slouched down in his favorite chair in front of the TV. His feet were propped on a footstool. The volume was on low. A half-empty can of beer dangled from his right hand, rocking between his forefinger and his thumb. He could hear the water running in the bathtub, which, he decided, was his main problem.

It was impossible to focus on the detective program with Sassy in the house. What a stunner she was. With her long legs and beautiful face, she was as pretty a woman as he'd ever seen, and he'd seen a lot of pretty women, not that he'd had much time for them.

Sassy was younger, softer looking, than he imagined a model with so many years of experience would be. There were no hard edges to her. He imagined her lying in the tub, her head leaning back, her eyes closed.

He'd never seen eyes that particular shade of turquoise. They deepened to a teal blue when she became frightened. He'd first noticed it when Buster had charged off the porch. She'd clung to him, and Lord help him, it had felt good. Too good. He imagined her rising from the tub, droplets of water clinging to her naked form. He imagined . . .

Knock it off, he furiously told himself, putting the can of beer to his lips and finishing it in two long swallows. Either there was something wrong with the beer, or his powers of concentration were slipping. Try as he might to block out the image, Sassy came swimming back in front of his eyes.

He angrily kicked away the footstool. He couldn't relax, knowing she'd be sleeping in the bed he'd intended as his marriage bed. Now there was a cruel twist, he thought, pulling back the tab on another beer, taking a long swallow. There was something too ironic about a beautiful stranger initiating the very mattress on which he'd planned to begin a family.

Of course the problem had been that his intended bride had run away the first time she'd seen the ranch. Luke squeezed the empty tin can into an hourglass shape.

So much for love, dreams . . . and reality.

Reality was Sassy of the golden hair and flashing eyes, of the long legs and firm high breasts, sleeping in his bed.

As long as Sassy remained a guest in his house, he was determined to show her his good side. In the morning when he woke her at five, he would thoughtfully bring her a cup of coffee. Models were always watching their figures, so it stood to reason that Sassy probably drank it black. It would be a nice touch to let her finish drinking her coffee first. Then he'd casually inform her the men had slept in the bunkhouse the previous night, and they would be joining them for breakfast. All ten of them.

He sipped more of his drink. He prized people with a generosity of spirit. Not many people had it. Still, Sassy had offered to cook, so he would graciously set the table. There wasn't much to setting a table. Everyone helped himself from the silverware in two big mugs in the center. It was the gesture that counted.

He'd suggest she eat first to keep up her strength. She needed to put on a few pounds, but not much. She'd felt pretty good to him.

Too good.

He'd be sure to compliment her and to pray she knew how to make biscuits and gravy the way the men liked them. He'd have a mutiny on his hands otherwise. They insisted on lots of gravy to go with the ham, steak, potatoes, and bacon and eggs.

Chester and the boys damn well better compliment her, too, or he'd break their stupid necks.

Cooks that looked as delectable as Sassy weren't the norm around the ranch, or anywhere nearby, for that matter. He hiccuped. The empty beer can joined the others.

He resolved to stay as far away from her as politely and humanly possible. She'd just have to understand what a busy man he was. Yes, that's exactly what he'd do, he decided.

But what would she do to keep from getting bored? Then he grinned as the perfect solution to his problem popped into his head. He wanted Sassy to get bored. Then she'd leave. It shouldn't be too hard. She was used to a fast-paced life. On that happy thought Luke dragged the back of his hand across his mustache, wiping off stray drops of beer.

He wondered whether Buster was in the bathroom keeping her company, or if the two of them were in the bedroom by now. If he knew Buster, that miserable dog had his head on the pillow next to hers.

Luke forced his attention back to the set. The television program had been interrupted by a commercial. He waited to see what garbage would be pitched this time.

What he saw on the screen had him on the edge of his chair. He shook his head as if to clear it, not believing what was before his eyes.

Sassy, in a skintight, beaded turquoise dress, her hair in a sophisticated chignon, was seated at a table in a posh restaurant. Her escort, a man in a tuxedo, was seated across from her. In a graceful gesture she lifted her hand to toy with the stem of her wineglass. The diamond bracelet on her wrist winked in the light. With a long manicured red fingernail, Sassy crooked her finger.

Luke sat on the edge of his seat, mesmerized, transfixed by the seductress on the screen. Was this the same Sassy who had clutched his neck when she'd been frightened? Was this the same girl who had begged him to let the dog be her companion so she wouldn't be afraid? Was this the same, innocent-looking Sassy who had tried to hide the fact that she'd been positively petrified when he'd told her their bedrooms adjoined?

If it was, this Sassy was a consummate actress. He didn't know which was the real Sassy. The Sassy on the screen was a self-confident vamp, easily wrapping her prey around her little finger. She pouted. She gazed at her partner through a thick curtain of lashes. She deliberately flicked out her tongue and ran it around the rim of the champagne glass in her hand. Luke could almost see the steam rising from the set.

When she dipped her head slightly, smiling seductively as the camera zoomed in for a close-up, Luke opened his shirt collar. It had to be one of the sexiest scenes he'd ever witnessed. There was Sassy slowly blowing out the flickering flame of the candle. She lowered her lashes again, but not before she sent a message no man in America could misinterpret.

Luke wouldn't be surprised if every woman in the country rushed out to buy Lady Exquisite cosmetics. By the time the commercial ended, he was sweating. If she could emote such passion in a one-minute commercial, after one movie, she'd be a star, he thought. Without one word of dialogue she had lit up the screen with her presence.

Luke sat back, willing his breath to return to normal. So, he reasoned, if she was destined for stardom, it would be a waste of his time and energy to imagine her lying in the bed fifteen feet away from his room. A terrible waste, he thought, pragmatically.

Three hours later, wide awake, he lay in bed, congratulating himself on his decision to banish Sassy from his mind. Buster trotted in and sniffed his face.

The damned dog smelled of wildflowers.

Moonlight streamed through the curtains. Sassy pulled the blanket higher. On the first day of her vacation, she'd met a man unlike any other. He was tough and foreboding, gentle and caring, and humorous. He was also disturbingly complex.

Yawning, she closed her eyes. The last thing she thought of was that she and Luke were the only two people in the house.

The alarm's shrill ring woke Luke. In one fluid motion he rolled out of bed. Pulling on a worn pair of jeans and shrugging into an old work shirt, he headed for the bathroom to begin his daily routine. Turning on the cold water faucet, he liberally splashed his face, shivering from the shock of the icy water.

"There's gotta be a better way," he mumbled, shuddering. He hopped back into the room to slip on his socks and his boots.

No matter how hot it got in the desert during the day, the nights were cold. And last night his bed had been colder than usual. Buster had spent the night with Sassy, depriving him of added warmth at the foot of his bed.

"Damned dog's a traitor," he muttered, returning

to the bathroom to shave. "Bring one pretty girl into the house, and he acts as if he doesn't know me."

Not that Luke blamed him. If he'd had the choice, he'd rather have slept with her too. Except, of course, he'd taken a solemn oath to leave well enough alone and never have anything to do with another actress.

Rubbing the dark stubble on his face, he started to reach for the shaving lotion in the medicine cabinet. His hand stopped in midair as his gaze swept past the toothbrush holder, then swept back.

Sassy had invaded his territory. His private male territory.

A pink toothbrush hung next to his beige one.

A woman's electric shaver lay side by side with his.

Two hairbrushes, one with strands of blond hair and one with strands of dark hair, were lined up like bookends.

Luke shook his head at the strange array of little plastic jars with colorful lids. Curious, he opened each one and sniffed. "Women," he muttered, taking one last sniff.

Even her perfume bottle was shaped like a woman, he noted. His finger ran over its dark blue form. Intrigued, he lifted the crystal stopper. Sassy's scent filled the room. He capped the bottle quickly and began to shave. He slapped lotion on his face, then swiveled to pick up a towel. "Geez," he said through clenched teeth.

If his eyes weren't deceiving him, he was staring at leopard print bikini panties and a matching bra trimmed in black lace.

And it was drying on *his* towel.

Impulsively, he reached out to touch the flimsy fabric. She was small all over, he realized. She had a small cute tush—he knew that from having picked her up so many times—and small luscious breasts, which he'd felt against his chest when she'd flung her arms around his neck when Buster had flown off the porch. Rules, he grumbled to himself, yanking open the linen closet for another towel. A man's gotta live by his rules.

He wouldn't allow another woman into his life or his bathroom.

After breakfast he would inform Sassy she'd have to rinse her things out early in the day. She could hang them outside.

Out of his sight.

Where he wouldn't have to be reminded of the feel of the fabric and imagine it on her skin.

His job, the way he saw it, was to eat fast, work on the fence all day, come home, work with the men fixing machinery, eat dinner, work on the books, then go to bed.

Her job, as long as she was there, was to cook breakfast until Maria returned. And she could brood or do whatever else she wanted to, as long as she kept out of his way. After all, he'd never promised Peter he would provide entertainment for her.

Luke combed his hair. Satisfied with his directive's to himself, he stepped out of the bathroom to wake Sassy. His men expected to eat by six A.M. They'd be in the kitchen on the dot of six, hungry and grumpy, the way they usually were until they'd had their coffee.

He opened the door to Sassy's room, his gaze focusing on the sleeping form in the bed. Buster raised his head from his place at the foot of the bed, saw Luke, and meekly jumped down. But Luke wasn't looking at Buster. His attention was riveted to the woman sleeping peacefully beneath the covers, surrounded by a field of cabbage roses.

Faint streaks of dawn were breaking over the mountains, casting enough light for him to see her hair fanning out on the pillow, her thick lashes curving impudently on her high cheekbones, her slightly parted dewy lips. He could also see the outline of her figure beneath the blanket—which instantly reminded him of the lingerie drying on his towel in his bathroom.

A ranch boss's main responsibility was to the men who worked for him. He had to take care of their needs so they could take care of his cattle. Considering it from that angle, he realized the laundry lines were too close to the bunkhouse. If those cowboys saw the little bit of nothing Sassy wore under her dress, they might start wondering about how she looked with nothing on. After all, he was wondering, and he certainly wasn't interested in her.

Knowing the men as he did, one thing might lead to another. It wouldn't be fair, what with them leading such solitary lives and all, he thought. Three days off a month to do some hell raising didn't amount to much.

He saw his responsibility clearly.

He'd have to cancel the directive he planned to give Sassy.

He'd just have to put up with seeing her lingerie in the bathroom along with her pink toothbrush, her cosmetics, her silly little electric shaver, the blond strands of hair in her brush, and her wildflower perfume.

Sassy had insisted she wanted to experience life on a ranch. He'd give her two days tops. But first he had to wake her up.

Coffee. He remembered his resolve to bring her a cup of coffee in bed. He dashed out of the room and into the kitchen to put on the kettle. He also filled the forty-cup percolator and plugged it in. In less than three minutes he returned to her room with a cup of instant coffee.

Luke noticed that Sassy had shifted position. Now she lay on her side, her profile outlined against the pillow. For a moment he couldn't resist watching her. He set the steaming cup of coffee on the night table.

"Sassy." He gingerly sat down on the bed.

"Go away."

Luke gave her shoulder a gentle shake. "Sassy, wake up."

She burrowed deeper under the covers.

Luke lowered his face near hers so she could hear him.

"Sassy, wake up."

He was rewarded with a tiny puff of breath and a whiff of her delicate perfume. He gritted his teeth, resolving to phone Maria and tell her if she valued her job, she had to come home immediately. He'd be glad to pay for someone to help her sister.

"Come on, Sassy, it's time."

"No, honey," she mumbled. "You come to bed. Let's make love."

Her invitation washed over him like warm honey. He sat up, forcefully tamping down his unwanted desire. This wasn't the way the script read, nor the way he intended to play it. Sassy couldn't be responsible for anything she said in her sleep. Unless, he thought with a pang of unwelcome jealousy, she regularly invited strange men into her bed.

"Wake up, Sassy," he said brusquely. "It's time for breakfast."

Sassy slowly turned over onto her back, giving him a glimpse of a pink nipple beneath her gown. Every nerve in his body tingled. He reluctantly realized it wouldn't take much to put a muzzle on his code of ethics. He didn't intend to spend another night counting mooing cows to fall asleep, when he could be with Sassy, satisfying his desire. Don't be an idiot, he cautioned himself. He'd been burned once by an actress. The next time he'd be asking for it with his eyes wide open.

Before Luke had time to dwell on his dilemma, one lovely turquoise eye blinked open, then the other. Both eyes were trained sleepily on Luke. "What are you doing here?" she mumbled, barely coherent.

Although Sassy was an early riser, she'd always been a reluctant one. It took four alarm clocks, a radio that blasted music in her ears, and three phone calls from her friend Beth to wake her. Sassy closed her eyes.

Luke lifted a brow in amusement, shaking her until she opened those fabulous eyes again. Luke grinned. Sassy was gloriously disoriented. She hadn't the faintest idea she had offered her body to him.

"What do you think I'm doing here? It's time to rise and shine, princess. That is, if you still want to keep your promise."

"To do what "

"To make breakfast. Frankly I don't think you have what it takes. You city girls are all alike." He let that comment hang in the air, wondering what he would say if she asked him in what way.

"Ugh." Recollection came slowly to Sassy. Her internal clock protested, but when reality worked its way into her brain, she smiled, and his heart lurched. It was bad enough seeing all her undergarments in his bathroom and wanting to have the pleasure of peeling them off of her, not his towel rod. But Sassy in dishabille was a sight that would tempt any man.

"Morning," she whispered drowsily, her voice raspy with sleep. "What time is it? I was having such a lovely dream."

So was he. He held her robe in front of him to hide the evidence of his lovely dream. "It's five o'clock."

She stifled a yawn, then raised her arms above her head. "Oh, gosh. Have I slept the day away? I guess I was more tired than I thought."

"You haven't slept anything away. It's five o'clock in the morning."

For a moment she stared at him as if she were

struggling to comprehend what he'd said. When she finally did, her reaction was instantaneous. She flipped over onto her stomach, plumping the pillow beneath her cheek. She was on vacation. Breakfast, served in bed by him at eleven o'clock or later, was more appropriate. The hell with foolishly made promises, she thought.

"Up."

"Are you crazy?" she said with a groan.

Entranced by the golden flow of hair rippling across her neck and shoulders, Luke was beginning to think so, especially since the bed looked so inviting. Sassy's foot hung drunkenly over the edge of the bed. Lovely foot, he thought. He'd like to taste it. It led to other enticing areas on her sensuous body.

He sat down on the bed. The springs creaked. "Think what your life would be like if you came through here on a covered wagon. I'll have you know this area was the site of the Goose Creek–Humboldt Emigrant Trail."

She waved her hand. "Go away. I don't want a history lesson."

He chuckled. Unable to resist, he lifted her hair to whisper in her ear. "Can't. You promised to make breakfast. It's getting late. The cows are already up."

"Tell them to sleep late," she groused, half turning onto her side.

"I told you you couldn't take it. Must be a trait common to city girls."

His challenge set her teeth on edge. "All right, you stinker. Give me a few minutes. I'll be right there."

"Coffee's on the night table. I hope you drink it black."

"That's very sweet of you," she said in a mocking tone.

"Part of the service, ma'am. Hurry up. I'll see you in the kitchen. Oh, by the way, did you know you talk in your sleep?"

Her friend Beth had once told her the same thing. "I never spoke in my sleep in my life," she lied, then asked, "What did I say?"

He grinned, wondering how she'd react if he told her. "Nothing really. I couldn't make out a word."

Four

Sassy knew she must have been crazy to offer to make Luke's breakfast. No sane person ate at five A.M. They might get up at that hour, but they didn't *eat*. Stomachs didn't work before nine in the morning, she told herself.

She hung onto the basin in the bathroom, staring at herself in the mirror. Her eyes were barely open. Her hair, which had always been heavy, tumbled down her shoulders in wild disarray. There was no time for her to do anything with it except run a brush through it. She quickly rinsed her face and brushed her teeth.

She put on a pink mini skirt, then threw a long, bulky crimson sweater over it. The sweater fit her like a nightshirt, hiding all but the hem of her skirt. On every trip, no matter how thoroughly she thought she'd packed, she always forgot something. This trip she'd forgotten her everyday jeans.

The only pair she had packed were designer jeans

that had caused a sensation in the fashion world. With her long legs and lively personality, she'd been the spokesperson for the line. Business had skyrocketed for the company.

The sides of the pant legs were studded with rhinestones, which were also smattered across the rear pockets. This particular pair had been designed and cut especially for her to wear in a national campaign. A cropped top, which featured fringes studded with tiny rhinestones, went with the jeans, but they were hardly appropriate for frying bacon and eggs for Luke at five-thirty in the morning. Later on she'd go into town and buy several pairs of regular blue jeans.

Sassy walked into the kitchen just as Luke was bending down to pick up a fork that had fallen onto the floor. Through his shirt she could see the rippling muscles across his broad shoulders. His hips were trim, his buttocks lean. Waking up to find him seated on her bed had rattled her more than she'd let him know.

She had dreamed during the night. She vividly remembered a tall strong cowboy with dancing dark eyes and devilish dimples invading her dreams. Luke fit that bill to a T.

She'd always been an excellent judge of character. There were too many men who thought all models were promiscuous. In her case, as in most others, that was far from the truth. The men she might have been interested in often shied away. It was the old story of the beautiful woman who spent lonely Saturday nights curled up with a book or went out to dinner with a girlfriend. The previous night she'd slept only a hairbreadth away from Luke's bedroom, and she'd had a wonderful sleep. This said something about the master of the house.

Luke Cassidy was trustworthy.

"Man the battle stations," she grumbled to herself.

Sassy focused her attention on the scene before her. Piled high on the counter were flour, butter, milk, eggs, bacon, ham, steak, and onions. It was evident that Luke hadn't put away the perishables from the previous day. Appalled at the waste, she criticized him.

"Luke, do you realize the meat is probably spoiled. You forgot to put it away last night. If you didn't want to, I would have. I hate to see waste."

Luke cocked his head. He froze in the act of gathering fistfuls of knives and forks from the drawer. His plan to be on his best behavior flew out the window. If it were possible for Sassy to look more inviting out of bed than in it, she did at that moment.

She was all long legs and suggestion. He ignored her comment. In less than an hour, ten men would be treated to the same enticing view of her.

"You might be warmer if you wore slacks. It's pretty cold this time of the morning."

Sassy heard only the censure. "You haven't heard a word I've said. Listen, Luke, I got up in the middle of the night to make your breakfast. It's impossible to cook in this mess." She turned up her nose at the ham. "How can you eat meat at this hour?"

Luke grabbed the ham and dropped it onto the

counter. "I'm asking you politely to wear something else."

The kitchen was warm from the preheated ovens and from the Franklin stove in the corner. "I'm fine. Is there a dress code here for having breakfast?"

The smell of wildflowers wafted under his nose. "Meals are a communal affair," he said. "The men slept in the bunkhouse last night. There are ten of them. That's eleven men to feed. I just took the food out of the refrigerator. Believe me, I'm not interested in waste either."

Stunned, Sassy dropped into the nearest chair. She couldn't believe her ears. Eleven men . . . eleven hungry men . . .

As if it were a horrible dream, the staggering variety and quantity of food heaped on the counter took on a new and sinister meaning. Luke's shopping spree yesterday hadn't been a lark. It had been a carefully planned visit to the supermarket—in order for her to be equipped to feed an army!

"Do you realize there's enough food there for twelve Thanksgiving dinners? Surely eleven men can't eat all this at breakfast?"

Luke dumped a fistful of knives, forks, and spoons into a couple of chipped brown mugs on the redwood tables. It wasn't the way he'd planned it, but he might as well prepare her for the rest.

"The men work hard from sunup to far later than sundown. Ranching is not a nine-to-five job. My men don't need to go to a fancy gym to get exercise. Try roping a steer, or digging fence posts, or lugging bales of hay to the areas where the cows feed. Or try lifting a sick cow or assisting when there's a breech birth. These men need a lot to keep them going. What's more, they expect biscuits and gravy too. I sure hope you know how to make them. If you don't, I'm going to have my hands full trying to learn in the next half hour."

Sassy's jaw dropped. She'd never made a biscuit or a pan of gravy in her life. "You mean Maria gets up every morning at five to cook all this?"

"Cheerfully," Luke stated, his polite intentions buried by his spiraling temper. Nothing was going right. Not since he'd first laid eyes on Sassy. Not since he'd picked her up and lifted her into and out of his pickup. Not since he'd seen her on the commercial. Not since his bathroom had been invaded. Not since she'd spoken in her sleep and had asked him to make love to her.

Especially not since then.

All he could think about was what it would be like to be under the covers with her. He wanted to watch her eyes as he took her over the top. He wanted to have her mouth tremble under his as she gasped his name. He never pretended to be a Boy Scout, and to be around Sassy and not want her, a man would have to be an Eagle Scout. On top of that she was incredibly sweet—when she wasn't fuming mad.

Sassy was fuming mad. She couldn't understand why he spoke to her as if she didn't have a compassionate bone in her body. What happened to the fun she planned to have on her vacation? Fun was possible on a dude ranch where the men would fawn over her. Fun wasn't possible while standing in a kitchen arguing with a rude cowboy who demanded that she change her clothes and then prepare an instant twelve-course morning feast. Maria must be an overworked saint, she thought. She couldn't wait to meet her and tell her to go on strike.

Luke regarded Sassy impassively, straining himself not to grab her arms and haul her to him. "It's my fault. I never should have expected you to be able to do this. Go back to bed. I'll handle this."

Sassy wasn't going to let him think she couldn't hold her own. She'd show him she could do it, then that would be the end of it.

She rolled up the sleeves of her sweater. "Get out of my way, Luke Cassidy. Before this day is over, I'll have your men eating out of my hand, or my name isn't Sassy."

"Is that a bet?" he asked in a silky voice. "Because if it is, my money says you're all talk."

Sassy blithely accepted the challenge. "You've got yourself a bet, cowboy."

Luke's mouth slowly curved upward. He grabbed his jacket from the peg on the wall, whistling for Buster to get up off the floor. He shoved his Stetson on his head.

"When you're through cooking, put on a pair of jeans. I can't have my men all hot and bothered," he said without a hint of apology.

Only after the screen door banged shut behind him did she realize Luke had neatly finessed her into doing exactly what he wanted her to.

Surveying her battleground, she took a deep breath, then mentally listed the sequence in which the food had to be prepared. Think army, she told herself. This is K.P. cuisine, not gourmet.

Maria's kitchen was practical, she noted gratefully as she scrubbed and cut potatoes, leaving on the skin. Once that was done, Sassy hunted for a phone book. In no time she was having a friendly chat with the surprised and helpful chef at Hansen's Model A Truck Stop Restaurant.

He gave her his surefire recipe for biscuits and gravy. He also invited her to stop by his place, assuring her he'd be glad to sell her biscuits she could freeze.

Spurred on by Luke's challenge, Sassy cracked then poured six dozen eggs into the cake blender and started the machine. The goo had lumps of white in it, but she was in too much of a hurry to worry about it. "This is a cholesterol nightmare," she said as the aroma of sizzling bacon turned her stomach.

Scant seconds later she drained the half-fried bacon onto paper towels and shoved the cut-up potatoes into the fat to fry. Next she separated the thick slices of the precut, precooked, smoked ham Luke had purchased. At the time she'd thought the price extravagant, now she saw it as a godsend. She shoved the steaks under the broiler.

Dirty pots and food-stained dishes were piled on every available counter. That didn't bother her one whit. The deal was that she make breakfast. It didn't include cleaning up. In fact, she had a few ideas of her own on how to pay back her sneaky host. For the next few days she'd do his bidding. After all, she was his guest.

She took a great deal of satisfaction in having everything ready on time. Or mostly ready if the men didn't look too closely. Inwardly she glowed with pride over her accomplishment. "Six A.M. and all's well," she said out loud. She grinned mischievously. "Now it's my turn."

She dashed back into her room, thankful for her training in fast clothing changes. After slipping into her fancy jeans, she flew into the bathroom.

She tipped her long curly lashes with dark brown mascara, stroked pink lipstick on her lips, and dabbed more perfume behind her ears and on her wrists. Luke had his little ways of playing a game, and she had hers.

She piled her hair in two expert twists high on her head, then artfully arranged long blond curls to frame her face. Stepping back to view herself in the mirror, she decided she was as ready as she'd ever be. When Sassy strolled into the kitchen, she looked like the high-priced model she was.

The men gaped at the beautiful apparition who would be serving them their breakfast. Chester, the burly foreman, introduced himself first. He had a thatch of red hair, a barrel chest, and a shy smile. Instinctively, she knew that she'd like him.

The motley crew ranged in age; she judged the youngest to be in his early twenties and the oldest in his late forties. The names Sassy heard mentioned belonged in a Western: Jack, Homer, Trace, Pistol, Yancy, Meriman, Bubba, Nolan, and Junior.

No one bothered to clarify who was who in the cast of characters, or who Junior was a junior to. She didn't bother to ask Luke. She was too aware of his powerful masculinity and his disapproving scowl. If looks could kill, she thought.

Sassy tried her level best to ignore him as she greeted each man. It wasn't easy. From the moment he stepped into the room it had been impossible to overlook him. She glanced up to find his brows knit in consternation, his lips set in a thin line. She gave him her best blank look, then turned to the others and poured on the charm.

Sassy was an expert in pouring on the charm. She made sure she stood close enough so each man got a whiff of her perfume, then she innocently waved her hand, knowing Luke was ready to pounce.

"That's enough with introductions. Let's eat," he ordered. Sassy, ecstatic at his irascibility, complimented herself on her progress. So far so good.

She purposely disregarded his barking edict. Instead, she began by greeting each man with a speech she'd rehearsed while changing her clothes. "The cows can wait another five minutes, don't you think?" What Luke thought was clearly written on his face.

"You have no idea how I admire real he-men like you," she said, her gaze lingering on each one's face in turn. "Back where I come from all the girls think the word cowboy is synonymous with tall strong men and romance."

A row of male chests puffed with pride. They gazed at her in admiration, hoping to hear more. Luke growled in her ear. "Cheap shot."

She turned so that only he could see her face. "I do what I can," she said, batting her lashes, but the look he returned was so heated, so evocative, she was incapable of coming up with a wise remark.

Chester was the first to snap out of his daze and hang his hat on the rack. Hesitantly, he held out his calloused hand.

"Thank you, ma'am. It sure is nice of you to fix our breakfast with Maria gone and all." His voice softened when he mentioned Maria's name. Sassy assumed he missed the regular cook.

She smiled into his brown eyes and heard Chester gulp. His face turned beet red to match his shirt. From the corner of her eye she saw Luke nudge the man closest to him. It started a ripple of thank-you's.

"Sit down, please," she said, deciding to go to phase two. It was all the men needed to hear. They lifted their legs over the bench seats in unison, then made a grab for the center of the table and the mug holding the utensils.

Sassy smiled. "So? What would you like first?" she asked, bringing over two jugs of juice.

Behind her Luke touched her arm. She whirled around to find him regarding her thoughtfully. How could his mere presence, his slightest touch, make her react so? "What?" she asked him.

"I think the men are used to eating everything at once. It saves time."

"Oh," she said, catching on. She'd been trying to find a way to prevent Luke from sitting down to eat. His statement gave her an idea. "Of course. Would you mind helping me serve?"

He nodded, then brought the heaping platters of food to the table. No one spoke as helping after helping disappeared before her eyes. They put pools of brown gravy over everything; bacon, eggs, and steak—all disappeared from view. The men noisily attacked the food, dousing the biscuits in the gravy.

Junior, a young man in his early twenties with a thick mop of blond hair, blue eyes, and sun-bleached eyebrows, finished first. He sat back, burped, and took a toothpick out of his shirt pocket. He started to pick his teeth.

Luke tapped his shoulder. "Junior, see you a minute?" Luke didn't wait for an answer. He nodded curtly, then strode briskly out of the room with the perplexed young man following.

When they returned the toothpick was nowhere in sight.

Yancy scratched his chest with both hands. "Outta' gravy," he said.

Luke laid a firm hand on Yancy's shoulder. Scowling, he jerked his head in Sassy's direction. At the time she was removing another batch of biscuits from the oven. Leaning over, she gave Luke another score to settle with her later. She deliberately and purposefully strained the limits of his patience.

Sassy brought the biscuits to the table. "Did you ask for something, Yancy?"

Luke hovered nearby. "Yes, ma'am. Is there any more of that delicious gravy? Please." Luke moved away, as if to say, "Yancy, you passed this time. Don't let it happen again."

Then Bubba almost knocked over Meriman's coffee cup as he made a grab for the latest batch of biscuits. Luke tapped him on the shoulder. Bubba soon followed Luke into the other room for a minute.

"Best gravy I've ever had, Sassy. Sorry for being clumsy," Bubba said as he sat down again.

She felt as if she had passed a major hurdle. She was glad they liked her cooking, but she wasn't ready to give credit to the helpful chef she'd called. Not with Luke waiting for her to make a mistake. "Why, thank you, Bubba. You and the boys have made my day."

"Sure is delicious."

"I'm so glad you like it, Meriman," she said. "I'll be sure to make extra gravy for you tomorrow." She winked at Luke. He rolled his eyes.

A chorus of praise for everything she cooked followed. Beaming, she promised each man a special treat. She also promised herself to make sure the food was done next time.

She glanced up at Luke to see a muscle working in his jaw. "Luke, if you're not too hungry, why don't you wait a minute and we'll eat together?"

Between ordering the men to quit belching, burping, scratching, and watching Sassy parade around the room, he hadn't dared take the time to sit down with them.

"Okay," he said.

He realized he had been looking forward to eating with her. "Chester, as long as you and the men are finished, you don't have to wait around. I'll catch up with you. Jack, Homer, you two are spending the night in the line shack. There are ample provisions there." The men thanked her again. After they left, Sassy whirled around to Luke, her eyes gleaming with pride.

"They enjoyed my cooking, didn't they?" She wanted to shout, she was so proud of herself. "How about those biscuits and gravy? Did you see Trace turn the gravy boat over to get the last drops?"

A flicker of admiration crossed Luke's face. He had to hand it to her. Not only was she gorgeous, but in ten minutes she'd had the men eating out of her hands. He'd never expected that feeding a bunch of well-meaning slobs would turn her on.

"Look at the table," he said, answering her question.

Sassy saw the empty platters. "Tell me the truth," she said excitedly. "Would they eat anything?"

He rocked back on his heels, studying the picture she made. Her cheeks were flushed a warm pink, her turquoise eyes sparkled, there was a streak of flour on her forehead. The curls bouncing around her face made her look like a saucy minx. She didn't look one bit like the sophisticated model he'd seen on television. How long would it take the ranch hands to make the connection, he wondered.

"Just about," he said.

"Nails?" she asked. "They'd eat nails?"

"Yup," he said, grinning and feeling relieved the men were out of the house.

"Oh, you. They adored my cooking, and you know it." Laughing, she swatted him with a dish towel, then winced in pain.

The smile on Luke's face instantly disappeared. His hand snaked out to capture hers. He turned her palm over and he frowned. "You were careless. Why didn't you wear gloves to protect yourself?"

"I couldn't find them." Tears sprang to her eyes. His size and air of righteousness galled her. It was her thumb that got burned, not his. Furious with herself for crying, she pulled her hand away, biting down on her lip from the sudden pain. He grabbed her wrists and jerked her to him.

"You burned yourself. You're not used to this."

"You're amazing," she said. "You act as if most women are used to serving an army. Well, I've got a flash for you, Lone Ranger. Most normal women in America aren't."

The tears were more than he could take. "Sassy, I'm sorry for jumping down your throat. It's just that I didn't like seeing you hurt on my account. The meal was wonderful. You had the men eating out of your hands. Literally. I thought Yancy would flat out make a fool of himself. Chester was so flustered the first time he saw you, he turned fire-red. The only woman he talks to is Maria. Nolan and Pistol kept poking each other under the table every time you turned around."

"Then why are you making such a fuss, Luke?" She was sure he could hear the wild beating of her heart.

He gazed into her turquoise eyes, focusing on the diamondlike tears clinging to her lashes. He forced himself to think of the movie she was about to make.

"Because if you get hurt or burn yourself, you might hold up production on your movie. I should never have asked you to make breakfast."

There was more to it, but Sassy couldn't figure it out. He was treating a minor thing as if it were a major catastrophe.

"Luke, I'm a big girl. I've been working all my life. Nothing is going to happen to me."

"That's right," he insisted. "You're not going out there and do the dishes. Come with me, and I'll fix you up."

She waited patiently while he applied a ribbon of salve to the base of her thumb. She peered at him from beneath her lashes. "For your information, Mr. Cassidy, I never had the slightest intention of washing the dishes."

Luke's brows rose, disappearing beneath the hair on his forehead. He leaned against the washstand. He realized he'd made more of her burn than was called for.

"Is that so?" he asked, relaxing.

"Yup," she said smugly. His eyes went to her bare midriff and the shimmering rhinestones.

He stroked the side of her face. It wouldn't take much to inspire him to kiss her. "Think you're pretty smart, don't you?"

"Brilliant."

"And you're sure your hand is okay?"

"Count on it."

He tweaked her nose, congratulating himself for resisting those luscious lips. "Well, seeing as how you're so healthy and so brilliant, you can collect the eggs."

She gazed at his mouth, thinking how close they were, how easy it would be to lean forward. . . .

"What eggs?" she asked, breaking her train of thought.

"Remember the chicken coops I pointed out yesterday?" At the look of disbelief on her face he nodded. "Those eggs. The little suckers have to be collected every day. Otherwise their nice little mommies can't sit down. Since you're such an independent customer, you might as well add that to your list of chores. Think of all the fun you'll have."

"What about your breakfast?" she yelled as he walked away.

"I'll grab some peanut butter and jelly. The men may have cast-iron stomachs, but I don't. When I eat, I like my food cooked. But you get points for trying," he said, leaving her with her mouth wide open.

Five

Walking with a loose and easy gait, Luke led his horse out of the stable. He wore chaps over his jeans to protect his legs. His Winchester 30-30 rifle was strapped to the back of his saddle. Today he and Nolan and Bubba were going after a band of coyotes that had been killing some of his cattle.

Sassy looked out of the window to see Luke mounting up. "Oh, no you don't," she muttered, flying out of the house after him.

"Hold it right there, Luke Cassidy. Chickens are out of my league."

His head came around. Shifting his hips, Luke ignored her and gave his sole attention to her bare midriff. The rhinestone fringes dangling from the hem of her short blouse were like lighted pendulums twinkling in the sun. Behind them her skin was smooth and white.

He could handle coyotes and snakes. He could rope a bucking bronco. But he didn't know what to do with her. She disrupted his routine. Now she stood there, her hands on her cute hips, her eyes flashing. She had worked herself up into an adorable snit.

It might have been easier if she were the aggressive career woman he'd expected. In fact, he would have preferred it. For over a year he hadn't thought one way or the other about women, not seriously. When he wanted his needs satisfied, there were plenty of local ladies to oblige him. His life was neat and tidy and busy, the way he liked it. No commitment, no entanglements.

Sassy tugged at his pant leg to get his attention. "Luke, did you hear me?"

He moved his leg. The merest touch of her fingers set off his already inflamed libido. He was vulnerable. He hadn't known it, but she sure proved it. She'd set him up with her leopard-dotted undies, that sizzling commercial, and the way she'd waved her perfumed wrist under his nose at breakfast. He hadn't been able to get out of the house fast enough to suit him.

"Sure I heard you, even the damn chickens heard you. What's with you? You got a thing against hens?"

He infuriated her with his superior attitude. Her chin shot up defiantly. "I've never gathered eggs."

He shrugged his shoulders, feigning a nonchalance he didn't feel. "It's very simple. They plop. You pick. Never mind. I'll do it later. You're on vacation anyway. Take the pickup truck if you want and go into town and sightsee. There are plenty of casinos.

Go to the museum, if you're interested in the history of Winnemucca."

"That's not the reason I don't want to do it," Sassy explained, trotting to keep pace as Luke spurred his horse down the worn path. "Suppose I hurt them? I've never been around chickens, except for a baby chick once at Easter time."

Luke checked the reins. He cocked his head and studied her for a moment. The sun backlighted her hair, framing her face. When he saw her expression, he frowned. "You're serious, aren't you?"

She nodded. The stallion danced in step, and she backed up. "Yes."

Of course she was serious, he realized with a start. Why should he expect her to know the first thing about gathering eggs? She hailed from the big city, where everything magically appeared in boxes or packages or on television screens.

Television screens. He still had a blasted headache from all the beers he had drunk after watching her on the tube.

"In that case, I suggest you crook your little finger. If it works with men, it's sure to work with a bunch of stupid birds."

Sassy struggled to maintain her cool. She lost it as it dawned on her that Luke had seen her commercial and hadn't mentioned it. "You saw the commercial?"

He hadn't meant to let her know. "Yeah, I saw it."

"When?"

His jaw hardened. "Last night."

"Last night!" she cried, flinging out her arms. She

sidestepped a cactus. "Why didn't you call me? I haven't seen it yet."

His gaze raked over her body. "As I recall you were in the tub bathing."

Missing the surly inflection in his tone, hers was all business. "Which commercial was it? We shot two. Was it the one where I crook my little finger and kiss him till his socks curl, or the one where I crook my finger and don't kiss him?"

He steered the horse alongside the fence. "How should I know?" He was running out of patience. "I've got better things to do than monitor whether you did or didn't kiss someone."

She rested her foot on the bottom rail. Luke watched, mesmerized, as she lifted stray strands of hair away from her neck. There was a heat gripping his gut that had nothing to do with the hot dry weather.

"You'd remember," she said without a trace of coyness. "The kissing one is sexier. It'll sell more cosmetics."

You're right, he thought. He'd never forget how she looked poured into the turquoise sheath, leaning across the table at her date. "Last night's ought to sell a fair share."

She shrugged her shoulders and moved away from the fence. "Maybe. My mother likes the tame one better."

"What's your mom have to do with it?"

"Mother? She's my manager, has been all my life." Buster rubbed up against her leg. Without thinking she stroked the dog's fur. "I really wanted to see the commercial. I left New York before the final edit."

"I'll be sure to barge in on you the next time it airs."

The mere thought of Luke seeing her naked in the bathtub made her shiver. With his Stetson pushed back on his head, his full mustache, and his set facial muscles, he looked every inch the tough western cowboy.

She brushed her palms against her pant legs. "Look, is there anything special about collecting the eggs?"

He couldn't get over her. He purposely treated her rudely so she'd back off and leave him alone. Instead, this exquisite creature who looked like a sun goddess and was about to increase her name recognition and her bank account wanted pointers on how to collect eggs.

His eyes flashed fiercely. "Did that man turn you on?"

His question caught her by surprise.. "What man?"

"The one you were making goo-goo eyes at in the commercial?"

'Lester?" The idea seemed so preposterous, she laughed aloud. Luke sent her a gaze that held no warmth.

"Lester's a dear."

Luke arched a disgusted brow. "But?"

"But?" she asked, barely managing to keep her tempter in check. "There are no buts."

"Then what's wrong with him?" he asked, wondering perversely about the other men in her life who weren't "dears."

Sassy kicked at a pebble with her toe. She would have liked to kick Luke. "What gives with you? I'm talking about chickens, and you're talking about Lester. If you and your crowd expect eggs for breakfast tomorrow, I suggest you get off the subject of Lester and teach me what to do."

Luke fixed her to the spot with his eyes. "I don't give a damn about the eggs. How good a friend is Lester?"

"Oh," she said on an indrawn breath, lowering her lashes so Luke couldn't see her reaction. A tingle went through her.

"A very good friend," she said truthfully when she lifted her head. "On the day we shot the commercial Lester phoned Harkness Pavillion every chance he had. His wife, Hazel, was in labor with their fourth child. You might say he tore his lips from mine and dashed off the set to be with the woman he loves." She let that sink in. "Now, Mr. Cassidy, about those eggs . . ."

His smile was slow in coming, but when it did, her heart thrummed. He leaned over in the saddle, lowering his face to within inches of hers. The air heated with their mingled breaths. He tucked his finger under her chin, then in a brazenly arrogant manner he slowly slid his thumb back and forth over her lips.

"Tell you what, Sassy. You just look at those hens the way you did Lester, and you can bet they'll do anything you want."

"What would you do if I looked at you like that?" she teased, her voice a husky whisper.

It was a question that had occupied a good deal of his time the night before, earlier that morning when he'd awakened her, and later in the kitchen. Her invitation nudged him past the breaking point. He cursed under his breath even as he drew her to him. With the backs of his fingers he stroked her cheek, then glided his hand under the wisps of hair at her neck. Then, without warning, he lifted her off the ground and into the saddle, facing him.

"What—what are you doing?" she stammered, clutching his shoulders for balance. His mouth was a grim line.

"Giving you the answer to your question. You did expect one, didn't you? Wasn't that the reason for all this?"

She shook her head. "No I—"

He never gave her time to finish her statement. He jerked her to him, smothering her protest with a kiss.

Sassy wasn't prepared. Until now it had been a lark, a fantasy, an adventure to share with her friend Beth when she returned home. But nothing in her experience had readied her for dealing with a man as elemental as Luke.

He took her lips in a savage kiss, lighting fires in her shocked body. There was no part of her mouth he didn't explore. Only when he heard her whimper, only when her fingers dug into his back did he end the assault. He'd begun to feel so much—and he couldn't allow it.

Tearing his lips from hers, he lifted her up and off the saddle and put her down on the ground again. Stunned, she stared at him, momentarily robbed of speech.

Silently cursing Peter for getting both of them into this predicament, Luke vowed to get Maria back pronto, even if he had to drag her.

"Both of us wanted that, Sassy," he said in a dangerously cold voice. "Only get it out of your head that it's ever going to happen again. I'm not a good little boy. There'd be no director around to say, 'Cut,' and protect your precious virtue, so quit playing games. I make my own rules. If we made love, I wouldn't stop. I'd take you over and over again until I had my fill. So, if you're smart, don't look at me the way you did Lester."

Breathing hard, shaken by feelings she hadn't known she could experience, insulted by his condemnation of her, Sassy lashed out. "You call that a kiss? A kiss is something to be shared. That was a macho excuse for lust. You had no right—"

"Leave it alone, Sassy." Luke picked up the reins. His eyes were darker, more intense than she'd ever seen them. Silhouetted against the mountains, his features appeared as hard as the granite rock.

"We're each traveling on a different path. I've been where you're going. You're leaving, I'm staying. No two people could have more diametrically opposed professions. Trust me, I've had them both. In a couple of weeks you'll forget all about this. You'll be swamped with directors and producers who'll want to arrange your life. Just don't mess with mine." He spurred the stallion before she could answer.

Miserable, knowing he was at least half right, she watched him ride off until he was a blur in the distance. His words hurt, but she had been playing games. It wasn't chickens or eggs occupying her turmoil-filled mind as she slowly made her way back to the house with Buster. It was the cowboy who rode his magnificent brown stallion across the desert floor, kicking up dust clouds in his wake.

Sassy never knew chickens made such a racket. No wonder Maria wanted them away from the house. Besides clucking incessantly, there were so many feathers flying in the air, it looked as though a pillow fight had just taken place.

"All right you noisy birds, now hear this. I am a star, at least I'm going to be. If you don't believe me, ask Luke. He's got all the answers."

Luke. Every encounter with him left her unsettled and wanting more. If she were smart, she'd leave on the next plane. She'd be doing both of them a favor and probably save herself heartache.

Yet his kiss, as punishing as he'd intended it to be, held a trace of desperation. He'd broken off the kiss when it had started to become gentle, when she'd begun to respond, when she would have melted in his arms. He'd warned her fairly. A selfish man would not have done that. A selfish man would have tried to take advantage of the fact that they'd spent the night alone together in his house. More importantly, a selfish man would not have been as upset as Luke had been.

Luke Cassidy might know everything there was to know about horses and cows, but what kind of man admits to being affected by a kiss, then slams the door on a repeat performance?

A man who had been terribly hurt by a woman, she realized. A man who was afraid to trust, yet was trustworthy himself. A man who could show anger, yet worried if she burned herself. A man who made sure she was treated with respect, then brazenly kissed her until the blood in her veins heated to the boiling point. An intractable, irreverent, impossible, infuriating, irritating, wonderfully handsome, exciting, hard-nosed rancher by the name of Luke Cassidy. Whom she wanted to get to know better in spite of all the horrible things he'd said. Aside from all that had transpired between them, she knew he was a very special person.

She mopped her brow. She had changed into a pair of shorts and a T-shirt. It was hot in the long low coop. She gathered the eggs and placed the filled baskets near the door. She worked steadily, glad that her thumb no longer hurt.

She plucked feathers off her arms, blew a few out of her mouth, and giggled. If her friend Beth and her mother could only see her now, they'd have a fit. Her hair hung in damp waves, plastered against her neck and back. Sweat ran down the valley between her breasts. One of her nails was chipped. She looked more like a bag lady, she thought, than a big time model, and she didn't care. She didn't even mind cooking.

Whatever else might have happened since she'd met Luke, she hadn't had one palpitation, bit of dizziness, or feeling of faintness, since she'd arrived. She had slept like a log the night before. There was nothing better than waking up to see the mountains and, if she wanted to be totally honest, knowing that she didn't have to pose for hours at a time. Maybe that's what Peter had had in mind.

After putting the eggs in the refrigerator, she cleared the table and filled the dishwasher, again surprised she didn't resent it. It was true she'd teasingly informed Luke that she drew the line at cleaning up, but her conscience wouldn't let her leave the house with piles of dirty dishes in the sink and all along the counters.

For a while she considered Luke's offer to drive into town, then discarded the idea. She wanted to stay on the ranch and explore. Thinking about the cowboys who would troop home expecting dinner, she put up a huge pot of stew, using every vegetable she could find in the refrigerator and the freezer. She made extra batches of biscuits as she listened to Dwight Yoakam tunes on the radio.

What objection could Luke have, she wondered, if they at least got to know each other? After all, she wasn't signing him to a life sentence. The only hitch in her plan was that Luke spent a good deal of the time on his horse riding off somewhere. Therefore, if she were to become better acquainted with him, she had to learn to ride a horse first.

She washed and wiped her hands, then untied the towel she used as an apron and threw it into the laundry hamper. She grabbed two carrots out of the vegetable bin and headed for the stable. Her eyes adjusted to the dim interior. It took her nose a little longer. The smell was definitely not eau de cologne, but it wasn't too unpleasant. Her steps muffled by the straw, she quietly headed toward a stall.

The horse, a huge brown animal, lifted its head and eyed her quizzically. "Hello," she said softly. She timidly put out her hand to stroke his coat. "You're a good girl, aren't you?"

"She's a boy."

Sassy whirled. Damn! she swore to herself. She'd know that cocky baritone anywhere. Guiltily, she hid the carrots behind her back.

Luke stepped out of the shadows. His shirt was open to the waist, his sleeves were rolled up. Sweat beaded his forehead. There was something very arresting about seeing a man dressed in jeans with his shirt opened to reveal sweat-glistening muscles. He leaned an arm on the handle of a pitchfork, appraising her with a cool look. Sassy felt as if she'd been caught with her hand in the money till.

"Finished with the hens?" He reached behind her to snatch the carrots. "Nice of you to think I might need a snack."

"What are you doing in here?" she demanded. It infuriated her to know that he could be there watching her as if she were a thief, and she hadn't even heard him. "I thought you were gone for the day."

"Obviously." He twirled the carrots by the stems.

"Thanks, but I'm not hungry. Sinbad might be later. I'll see he gets them. As long as you're so full of energy, you can help me clean out the stalls."

Luke was insufferable. He knew why she was there. Why didn't he come out and admit it? "I've never cleaned a stall out in my life," she said haughtily.

His mustache twitched. His eyes reflected the light shining in the windows. "It's easier than collecting the eggs. All you have to do is make believe you're spreading fertilizer in a garden, only in reverse."

She wrinkled her nose. Some fun. "I don't see the need," she lied.

He chuckled. Darn if he didn't enjoy getting her goat. "If you don't believe me, better not back up." She froze in her place. She'd paid almost two hundred dollars for her Italian leather sandals. Luke laughed and took her arm. "Just teasing. Bubba and Nolan killed the coyotes before I got there, so I came back. I had a hunch if I left you, you'd get in trouble. How's your hand?"

She swatted a horsefly, making believe it was Luke. "Fine."

He licked his lips. "Good, then seeing as how you're itching to get a taste of real ranch life, you can help me. That is if a big-city model's not too fancy to do this kind of work."

Goaded, she grabbed the pitchfork. She regarded it as a foreign object.

"Spoiled your plans, did I?" There was a facsimile of a smile lurking around the corners of his lips.

"I don't know what you mean."

"Sure you do, but we'll leave it for now."

Luke showed her how to clean out the stalls. After half an hour she was exhausted and didn't care if he knew it. As far as she was concerned she'd proven her point. Nevertheless, she hid her hand, putting a brave smile on her face to hide a newly forming blister.

Luke's eagle eye caught the movement. Without asking he lifted it up in his, turned it over, and shook his head.

"City girl. Come on. It's more salve for you." He all but dragged her into the house to repeat the first-aid routine.

"Quit enjoying yourself," Sassy grumbled, but his hands felt nothing short of wonderful as he applied the salve to her blister.

"Then suppose you stop trying to ride Sinbad without my permission. If you think a few calluses on your hand are bad, they'd never match the ones you'd put on your backside." He shoved his hat back on his head and left her standing there.

She was too tired to think of horses or how Luke saw through her so easily. She was tense from the electricity that seemed to spark between them when he was near her. The man irritated her yet he drew her to him like a moth. Men usually treated her as some sort of unattainable star. Luke treated her as an annoyance, and she kept coming back for more. She had to be crazy to be interested in him.

She lay down to take a nap and dreamed about him. He was solicitous, attentive, kind, went out of his way to teach her how to ride a horse, then praised her for being the most apt pupil he'd ever had. In short he was everything he wasn't in real life. On top of that, there wasn't a pitchfork or a basket of eggs in sight.

At dinner time Luke helped her serve. She was very conscious of the way he kept looking at her. His hair was still damp from the shower. He smelled lemony and clean. He wore a pair of tan jeans and a white shirt with the sleeves rolled up. She waited for him to put food on a plate and eat, and it was a long time before he did so.

The men asked a whole host of questions about her work, the movie she was about to make, whether she liked the ranch, and whether life in the city really was as awful as they'd heard. Yancy mentioned he'd seen her commercial.

Sassy happened to be handing Luke the bowl to refill the stew when Yancy spoke. Luke's eyes narrowed and he seemed to be waiting for a comment that he might not approve of from one of the men. Sassy bit her lower lip to keep from smiling. Luke, she realized, had been watching her like a hawk, ready to pounce on any man who might step over the line.

She whispered, "Better be careful with that bowl, Luke. It's liable to break."

The men appreciated everything she cooked, and Sassy couldn't recall experiencing more camaraderie in her life. It was like being away at camp. The meal was accompanied by laughter, good-natured ribbing, and lots of praise for Sassy's efforts.

Not one man burped, scratched, or belched. No one wanted to break up the fun.

Homer rose, clinking his glass with a spoon. "Sassy, seeing as how you're so nice to us, the guys and I want to return the favor. Is there anything we can do for you?" A chorus of men echoed Homer's question.

Sassy glanced over at Luke, who was leaning against the counter, his legs crossed at the ankle. He hadn't participated in the conversation, but Sassy knew nothing escaped him. A slight nod of his head gave her permission.

She smiled at Homer. "I want to learn to ride a horse."

"I've reserved the pleasure of teaching her for myself, boys," Luke smoothly cut in. "Sassy, why don't you think of something else and let Homer know tomorrow."

She whirled around. Their gazes met in a clash of wills. Both knew that he'd never offered to teach her to ride. On the contrary, he'd done everything to prevent it. The undercurrent of tension between them went unnoticed by the others. Homer, aiming to please, offered another suggestion, one that was immediately seconded by the cowboys.

"A few of us fool around with the harmonica. The rest make believe they know how to sing. If you're not planning to do anything now, how about joining us in a little sing-along out on the porch?"

Sassy glanced over at Luke. She dared him to interfere. "What a wonderful idea!"

For the next hour, Sassy joined the men, her sweet lyrical sounds lifting above the deeper male voices. Luke joined them, too, adding his rich baritone.

Chester finally called a reluctant halt to the festivities, reminding everyone that the next day was a workday. Sassy, her face glowing with happiness, turned to Luke. "I think they're wonderful. Every last one of them."

Luke cleared his throat, and she saw his gaze drift down to her long bare legs.

"Sassy, it was very nice of you to make dinner," he began. "The boys and I really appreciate it."

Warmed by his praise, she was certain Luke had waited until the men had left to compliment her on the dinner. She wondered whether he would first praise the biscuits, the savory stew, or the way she'd set the table instead of dumping the utensils into mugs.

"I guess I was a little hard on you in the kitchen when you asked Homer to teach you to ride. Do you still want to learn?"

"I'd love to," she exclaimed, thrilled Luke would be her teacher, yet wondering why the look on his face didn't match his kind words.

"The boys won't be eating breakfast here in the morning. They're riding out very early."

"Oh."

"Nevertheless, when they're around, I'd appreciate it if you wore something more appropriate. I don't think they knew what they were eating or singing about tonight. They were too busy gawking."

Sassy's smile disappeared. She was so stunned at the unexpected insult that she glanced down at herself. Her blue top was scooped low, snug at her breasts. The very brief tan shorts, which were her favorite pair, hung just below her derriere.

As far as she was concerned she was properly dressed to sweat over a stove. There hadn't been an empty platter of food left on the table, which only proved Chester, Junior, Meriman, and the rest had paid more attention to their food and the lively conversation than her. Luke could take a flying jump!

She was growing angrier by the second. "Tell me, Mr. Cassidy," she said defiantly, her eyes flashing, "who set you up as an arbiter of fashion? What do you suggest I wear?"

There was a brief, pregnant pause in the conversation. Luke arrogantly shifted his gaze from Sassy's luminous eyes to her breasts and then back again. The expression on her face more than indicated she was daring him to make a remark. The fact was, he thought sullenly, *he* had been watching her all evening, wondering what it would feel like to kiss her breasts and have those long legs wrapped around him.

He was furious with himself for starting the whole thing. But he couldn't stop thinking of her in his bed. When he wasn't with her, he was thinking about her. When he was with her, he wished he were anywhere else. She continually set his teeth on edge.

Pushed past endurance, he snapped, "Anything but that."

Sassy exploded. "Oh, for Pete's sake!" If she didn't know better, she'd swear he was jealous. "Tell you what, Luke," she said. "I really appreciate your interest in what I wear. Why don't you come into my room tonight? I'll model my clothes. You can choose the ones you think are suitable." She started to walk away from him, but he caught her arm and whirled her around.

He lowered his face to within an inch of hers. "Don't push me, Sassy. If I came to your room tonight, you wouldn't be putting on your clothes because I'd be ripping them off."

Six

Neither Luke nor Sassy was ready for another confrontation.

For the rest of the evening Luke closeted himself in his study, failing miserably in his attempts to work. He lounged in his chair behind his oak desk, his long legs propped up on the top. Sassy had charmed the men with more than her good looks, he thought, then he mentally listed her good qualities.

For one thing she had a sense of humor and a temper, an unbeatable combination. She was witty and could hold her own, letting loose with a snappy wisecrack or a smoldering look. She'd bested him at his own game and brought out a fierce protective streak in him. Earlier she'd joined in the fun, singing with the men. He could tell she thoroughly enjoyed herself. Nothing about her was false. She was genuinely nice—which thoroughly annoyed him.

Every time he thought about the tempestuous beauty with her glorious golden hair tumbling about her shoulders, he sizzled with irritation. Peter had strained their friendship to the breaking point. What right did he have to foist her on him?

While Luke was silently abusing Peter, Sassy's ire was aimed toward Luke. The ranch would be perfect, she decided—if Luke were different. She liked the open space, loved it in fact. It was a far cry from the windy caverns of the city, there were no horns blasting all night long, no police sirens. Surprisingly she hadn't minded the physical work. And she'd thoroughly enjoyed the friendly discussions with the cowboys whose personalities she was beginning to appreciate. She'd especially liked singing with them after dinner.

What she minded was Luke.

She returned to her room, flouncing onto the bed, staring at the empty picture frame. The clue to Luke was in this room, she was sure of it.

She wrote a letter to Beth describing the myriad desert hues. "I'm going to buy a pad and sketch some designs." She tapped the pen on the pad. "The owner of this place doesn't remotely resemble the cowboys you told me about. He's cold, arrogant, and dictatorial. I can't for the life of me imagine what Peter sees in him as a friend." She chewed on the pen, then added, "But I'm going to find out."

She dashed a letter off to her mother, assuring her that she was getting ample rest. "Peter should be delighted." Exactly what he'd be delighted about, Sassy still had to figure out. Luke was an imperious, ungrateful fool. He was also maddeningly virile.

After her bath she rinsed out her lingerie, then

went downstairs and flipped on the TV in the living room. She finally saw her television commercial, watching it with a critical eye for imperfections in her delivery. Gradually, the combination of the day's activities and the quiet solitude of the desert lulled her into a relaxed state. Soothed, she retired for the night.

She dreamed about Luke. This time she was dressed in her new skimpy bathing suit and was standing on the porch. When he saw her, he ripped off his shirt, threw it around her shoulders, picked her up in his arms, and carried her off.

Unfortunately that was the point at which she woke up.

Still, if progress were measured in minuscule amounts, she was making headway with him. He was going to teach her how to ride.

The bright sunshine poured through the window. Dust motes bounced along with her as she jumped out of bed. For long moments she admired the beauty of the desert and its stillness, punctuated only by the chirps of birds. Glancing at the clock, she hurried into the bathroom to wash, dressing quickly in her designer jeans. Today she would go to town to purchase some practical ones.

In the kitchen, she poured a cup of coffee, buttered a roll, and began to munch on it when she spied the note Luke had left: *Be ready at 10 A.M. for your riding lesson.*

She gulped the last of the brew as she heard Luke's footsteps. Sassy leaped up from the chair. Chester walked in, slapping his hat on his thigh. Deep lines creased his craggy face. "Morning, Sassy. You ready?"

She smiled warmly at him. "For what?"

"Luke said to teach you to ride."

Her face fell. Luke hadn't broken his promise, he'd simply rearranged it so that he didn't have to be bothered with her. Sassy would have her riding lesson.

She pasted a bright smile on her face, walking side by side with Luke's foreman to the stable. She noticed he favored his right leg. "Are you all right?" she asked.

"Fine," he said with a grunt. Chester tilted back his hat and scratched his head. "You sure you want to do this? We could go to town if you like."

She swiveled around, skipping backward, smiling. "Positive."

He nodded in agreement. Everyone with half a usable brain, he thought, should know how to sit a horse—women included. "You sure you promise to mind me?"

"Absolutely." She clinched it by throwing her arms around him and kissing his whiskered cheek. "Chester, if you teach me to ride, I promise to bake you your favorite cake."

He wiped his cheek with his sleeve, embarrassed by her enthusiastic display of affection. His face turned as red as his hair, but his brown eyes lit up with anticipation. "Chocolate? Maria knows I like chocolate."

Delighted, Sassy pressed her palms together. Again she'd heard his tone soften when he mentioned Maria's name. "Double chocolate."

He smiled briefly, then pulled a serious face. He

shifted a wad of chewing tobacco to one side of his mouth.

"Okay, little gal. You've got yourself a deal. Now come on, and I'll give you your first lesson."

Chester threw a halter on the brown horse and led him out into the sunlight, heading for the corral. Sassy strolled along beside him, still concerned about his limp. "Does it hurt much, Chester?"

"Not as bad as it looks. I took a spill last week. It wasn't nothin', but Luke caught me favoring my leg. He's real fussy if any of us gets hurt. Sometimes too concerned to my way of thinking," he added.

"But isn't it good that Luke cares?" she asked.

Chester shifted the wad of chewing tobacco to the other side of his mouth. "I reckon."

Curious, Sassy asked, "How long have you and Luke been together?"

He rubbed his thigh. "Since the time we both were in Hollywood making pictures."

Her mouth dropped open. "You were in the movies too?"

"Yup. We did all kinds of things. Some of them pretty crazy. There were times we played both the Indians and the homesteaders in the same picture. One time we even had to shoot ourselves, playing both parts." Sassy was anxious to hear more, but Chester changed the subject.

"Listen up. I'm going to explain the basics to you first, then we'll put you on Sinbad. Mind you, he sometimes likes to do things his way, so listen close."

Sassy was grateful Chester treated her like a complete novice. Her total riding experience was limited to carousel horses and an occasional pony ride when she was a child. By the time Chester finished saddling the horse, Sassy knew the rudiments. "And always get on from the left," he said, tightening the girth and helping her up.

Chester adjusted the stirrups. He handed Sassy the reins. "We'll take it nice and easy the first time."

After a rather wobbly start, Sassy was able to maintain her balance in the saddle, though at times she felt like a human pogo stick. When she questioned Chester, he assured her that it would take time for a tenderfoot to get the rhythm.

"Don't complain. Sinbad's in a relaxed mood today. Be patient. It'll come to you."

Before long Sassy gained confidence. Anxious for Chester to rest his leg, she prevailed upon him for permission to try riding on her own.

"Lean against the fence and rest. Where could I go?" she asked, laughing happily. Sinbad snorted.

Chester rubbed his thigh. "Guess you gotta do it sometime. Hold his head up and kick a little harder. He's used to men riding him. Be more decisive."

"How about that, Chester, I'm riding." For the next ten minutes she bounced up and down, wishing she could look glued to the saddle the way Luke did earlier.

She glanced over at Chester. Buster was sitting by his side, playing with a rock. "Chester, don't be shy. If your leg is bothering you, I can stop now."

Chester stretched both arms along the top railing, propping his sore leg on the bottom rail. "Quit treating me like a baby. You're no better than Luke. Go on with your riding. You ain't saddle sore yet." His gaze never left Sassy as he gauged his pupil's progress.

"Okay," she called, tossing her hair over her shoulder, "but when you want me to stop, tell me, and I'll walk Sinbad over to you."

Sassy was on the far side of the large enclosure when the trouble started. She'd lost her initial trepidations, and relaxed her grip on the reins, relaxed her attention, waving proudly with one hand. Her timing couldn't have been worse.

Neither she nor Sinbad heard or saw the rattlesnake slither out from behind a rock. Its sudden hissing spooked the horse. Sassy lost control of the reins as the terrified horse reared up on his hind legs. Fear made Sassy's lungs feel as if they would burst in her chest. Petrified, she screamed, adding to the animal's fear.

"Try to grab the reins, Sassy," Chester yelled, hobbling and running as fast as his leg permitted.

Frantic, Sassy tried uselessly to follow his instructions. "I can't reach them."

Sinbad, sensing more trouble with an inexperienced rider on his back, stretched his neck out and took off as though his life depended on it. Sassy flew into the air, landing on the ground with a painful thud. She lay doubled over, the wind knocked out of her.

Chester dispatched the snake, then hobbled over to her. He knelt down, rubbing her hands in his. "It's all my fault," he said to the unconscious girl. "I never should have left you."

Neither saw the horse and rider galloping toward

To get a free *Loveswept* ®calendar, packed with information about *Loveswept* romances in 1990, simply fill out the form below.

*C*alendar available early December, 1989. Offer good while supplies last.

Name _____

Address _____

City _____ State_____ Zip _____

Would you please give us the following information:

Did you buy Loveswept Golden Classics (on sale in June)?
____Yes   ____No

If your answer is yes, did you buy __1   __2   __3   __4

Will you buy Golden Classics featuring Hometown Hunks on the covers?
I will buy 1-2____, 3-4 ____, All 6____ None____

How often would you like to have an opportunity to purchase Golden Classics?
Every month_____ If so, how many per month_____
Quarterly_____

* One calendar per household.

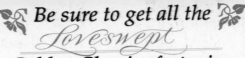

Be sure to get all the

Loveswept

Golden Classics featuring

HOMETOWN HUNKS

On sale in October

NO POSTAGE
NECESSARY
IF MAILED
IN THE
UNITED STATES

BUSINESS REPLY MAIL

FIRST-CLASS MAIL   PERMIT NO. 174   NEW YORK, NY

Postage will be paid by addressee

Loveswept

Bantam Books
Dept. CN
666 Fifth Avenue
New York, NY10103

them at breakneck speed. Luke, his face filled with fear, jumped off his horse and was beside Sassy in an instant.

"Call Jerry Marks. His number's in the book near the phone in my study. Tell him what happened and ask if he can come out to examine her. Then take my horse and get Sinbad back. Sassy'll be all right. She's more scared than hurt." In case she wasn't, Luke wanted Chester out of there. He couldn't take Chester blaming himself and trying to help Sassy at the same time.

"Sassy, can you hear me? Can you try to move your legs?" She whimpered, but the sound gave him encouragement. At least she didn't have a concussion. "Do it, honey. Try to do it for me."

Her eyelids fluttered open. She moved her legs.

Luke gave a huge sigh of relief. He expertly and quickly felt for broken bones. He removed his shirt, rolling it into a makeshift pillow for her head. She was bruised and would hurt for a few days, but there were no broken bones. She did have a cut on her leg, though.

Chester rushed out of the house. "Doc's on his way. Boss, I'm sorry. A rattler spooked Sinbad. Sassy lost control. It never would have happened if I'd stayed with her."

Luke thanked a higher being that Sassy had come to so quickly. "Forget it, Chester. Go get Sinbad. I'll take care of her."

Luke gathered Sassy to his chest, cradling her gently. Tears rolled down her cheeks. "Oooh, it hurts."

He kissed her forehead, forgetting his promise to

keep as far away from her as possible. "I know it hurts, sweetheart, but we'll have you fixed up good as new."

Even in her pain-filled state, Sassy felt his kiss, reveled in the change in him. He'd called her sweetheart and honey. His chest was warm and solid and comforting.

Dirt streaked her pale face. Her pant leg was ripped. "Luke," she said with a groan, "what are you doing here?"

"Hush, honey, don't talk," he said, blaming himself anew for her pain. He was supposed to have given her the lesson. She'd come close to getting seriously injured while in his care. He'd tricked her into cooking, collecting eggs, cleaning out the stall, and on top of that he'd acted like an idiot and yelled at her for wearing shorts.

"I forgot my wire snippers. I'm glad I did."

He was filled with remorse. When she'd asked for his help earlier, he had flung it back in her face with a stupid remark. But he wasn't sorry for kissing her. At least he'd have that much to remember after she left. He wouldn't blame her if she hated him.

He lifted her up in his arms, carrying her as though she were the most fragile flower in the world.

She tested her bottom lip with her tongue. "I feel as if I've gone ten rounds and lost. Will Sinbad be all right? He ran away."

He brushed away her concern. "Don't worry about Sinbad. Chester will bring him home and cool him down."

"I still want to learn to ride. Isn't it true you're supposed to get back on or you'll lose your nerve?"

"Don't even mention it." Luke stroked her back, reassuring himself she was in one piece. Once inside the house, he went into the den and laid her gently down on the couch. He adjusted the pillows behind her head, then removed her shoes. He saw that his hands were shaking.

"You could have really hurt yourself, or worse."

"Don't be angry with me," she mumbled. "The reason I wanted to learn to ride was so we could be friends. You were so angry last night. Ever since we met you've blown hot and cold toward me."

She was dead wrong. He'd been only one temperature. Hot. He could never be just her friend. Neither could he kick her out while she was down. If Sassy were naive enough to think he wasn't remembering how she'd returned his kiss, then he would have to be the strong one.

"Sassy, the hurt will pass. We all take a spill now and then. Tell you what. When you're feeling better, I'll take you for a ride, and we'll swim in the pool I told you about."

As he talked he gently unzipped her jeans, taking care to lift the material away from the cut on her leg. He realized again how glad he was that he'd ridden back for the wire snippers. If he hadn't helped her off with her clothing, Chester would have.

"Maria can sew the rip in your pants when she comes back tomorrow. She's terrific with a needle." With infinite tenderness he slipped the material down her legs. She was wearing pink bikini panties with butterflies on them. He cleared his throat, thinking he must be crazy for his prurient thoughts at a time like this. "You rest. I'll only be a minute."

Sassy closed her fingers around his hand. She was in too much pain to be embarrassed. "Luke, please don't blame Chester."

After his machismo display she probably thought he was an ogre. "If I'm going to blame anybody, it's going to be myself."

Sassy licked her lips. She'd managed to be a first-class nuisance. "I know I haven't let you work . . ."

Luke tucked a stray lock of hair behind her ear. "That's the understatement of the year," he said, purposely teasing to stop her from worrying.

Tears trickled down her cheeks mixing with the streaks of dirt on her face. "All I wanted was a little fun. I'm sorry. I'll leave in the morning."

"Shhh, we'll talk about it later," he said, blotting her tears with a tissue. "I never kick a wounded guest off my ranch. Especially when it was my horse that did the wounding." He patted her shoulder and rose. "Besides, what would your mother say if I sent the star back looking as if she belonged in a war movie? She'd probably come out here and kill me. So you see, you're going to stay right where you are until I say you're okay."

She sniffled. It felt so good to be pampered. "Don't tell me that just to be nice."

He smiled indulgently. "Me? Say something nice? Never." He hated seeing her in agony. "Don't move. I'll be right back."

"I couldn't move if I wanted to," she murmured weakly. "Tell Chester I still owe him a chocolate cake."

Luke returned to her side. "What for?"

"For teaching me how to ride Sinbad." She winced. "Oh, by the way, there's enough stew leftover for dinner."

His brows lifted. "You still thinking about cooking?"

She tried to nod and couldn't. "It's getting to be a habit."

Luke was silent for a moment, absorbing her pain and marveling at her generosity. He'd told himself she was just a model who had come to his ranch looking for kicks and a few laughs before going out to Hollywood to shoot the movie. What a fool he'd been.

When he spoke, his voice was gruff with emotion. "That makes us even, Sassy. Patching you up is getting to be a habit too."

Everything about her was getting to be a habit, he thought. If he weren't careful, he wouldn't be able to break it.

Jerry Marks examined Sassy. He pronounced her sore but whole. Jerry, a blond-haired daredevil, had arrived in Winnemucca five years earlier from Los Angeles, declaring he'd had it with big cities, smog, and traffic jams. Jerry's five-year marriage had gone sour. His attitude toward women was simple and straightforward. "I can't live with 'em and I can't live without 'em," he'd told Luke.

Luke walked his friend to his car. Jerry dug into his pocket for his car keys. "A good night's rest, a couple of rubs with Maria's secret liniment, and Sassy'll be fine. What's the story with you and her, or shouldn't I ask?"

Luke regarded him impassively. "Nothing. Sassy's a guest. Peter sent her for a little R and R."

Jerry slid behind the wheel. He'd known Peter for years. "Prettiest guest I've ever seen. Tell Pete to send me one too. On second thought, maybe *I'll* give her the liniment rub."

Luke gritted his teeth. For the first time he wanted to strangle his friend. Behind his joking he knew Jerry was serious. Jerry wined and dined and bedded as many women as his time allowed. He was charming, knew how to show the ladies a good time, and had the gift of gab, which Luke knew he lacked. But if anyone was going to touch Sassy in an intimate way, it sure wasn't going to be Jerry Marks.

Jerry turned the key in the ignition. "I can swear I've seen her someplace. What does she do?"

"Models," Luke said, slamming the car door.

Jerry nodded, looking thoughtful. Suddenly, his palm hit the steering wheel. "Hey, that's it. I saw her on television last night. She fogged up the guy's glasses." He made a motion with his hand, the kind men make to each other when they see a beautiful woman. "If you two don't have anything going, I'll stop over in a few days on purely personal business. She'll be ready to go for a ride by then." Seeing the hostility in Luke's eyes, Jerry grinned. "Then again, perhaps I won't. At least not till you make up your mind. But I warn you, old buddy, somebody's going to snap her up. Might as well be me." Chuckling, he roared off in his Porsche.

Luke muttered under his breath until the car was a speck of red on the road. Helping Sassy change into her lavender nightgown had been the hardest thing he'd ever done. She'd tried to modestly cover herself, not that it did much good, while he pretended not to be affected.

He had gazed at the satiny slope of her back, the small, delicate indentations along her spine, and the shape of her hips. Skin so soft should not be marred with scratches and black-and-blue marks, he'd thought. It should be kissed and fondled and cherished. Preferably by him.

But he wasn't going to do it. He'd had one devastating love affair. He couldn't afford another. He took the steps two at a time, hurrying into the house, stopping first for the liniment and a bath sheet.

Sassy eyed the jar in Luke's hand. Her hip throbbed. "What is that?"

"It's Maria's secret potion. Jerry thinks you'll benefit by her liniment rub. It works wonders on us."

Sassy rolled onto her stomach, lifting her hair over her head. "I'll try anything."

Nothing was going to make this easier for him, and the quicker he set about it, the faster he'd get out of the room. He slipped the blanket down to the end of the bed. Adjusting the bath sheet, he draped it over the lower half of her body. Sassy lifted up a fraction as he raised the gown to her shoulders. He put some of the scented lotion on his palms and touched her naked flesh.

His hands felt wonderful on her body. At first he touched her with feathery caresses, letting her get used to the pressure. As he felt her relax, he let his hands glide up and down her spine, kneading the soreness, drawing the ache from her bones. Sassy sighed in deep contentment. She'd had professional massages by experts in New York, Rome, Paris, and Los Angeles. But nothing could compare to Luke's expertise.

She floated in a state of sensual pleasure. Heat curled up from her womb, seemingly directed by the path of Luke's fingers. As he worked the healing balm into her sore muscles, she confessed, "I could lie here all day."

"Naturally," he said with a chuckle, trying not to kiss the hollow near her shoulder bone or the sides of her breasts, which were so evident.

Maria had mixed perfume into her secret lotion. The heady fragrance in the soothing lotion, combined with the effects of the medicine, worked to ease the tension. He massaged her legs and then each toe separately.

"Luke, I don't care what's in Maria's secret potion. Your hands are magic."

By dint of will, he forced himself not to think, not to want to lower his mouth and kiss each place his hands had roamed. He pressed down with his thumbs, moving up the backs of her legs, circling and massaging each muscle with long, soothing strokes. But as his hands began to knead close to her inner thighs, he trembled. Beads of perspiration broke out on his brow. When he could stand it no more, he said, "I think you've had enough."

He replaced the lid on the jar of liniment and patted Sassy's back and legs with the towels. He knew if he touched her a second longer, he wouldn't be responsible for his actions.

"You're not through already," she grumbled drowsily.

He pulled the blanket over her shoulders. "Get some sleep, honey. I'll be nearby if you need me."

Her arms hugged the pillow. "Mmmmm. Luke . . ."

He went to the window to adjust the amount of air and took a deep breath. "What is it, Sassy?"

"When you kissed me on the horse yesterday morning, it wasn't your fault," she mumbled. "I just wanted you to know that."

He clenched his fists. So she had been thinking about it too. The kiss stood between them like a dark secret, a moment of carnal lust. He couldn't get it or her out of his mind. He'd hidden away in his study the night before, pretending to work, when all the time he'd seen her face before him.

He went into the bathroom and splashed cold water on his face. Sassy's lingerie hung on the rack. Luke let out a groan of frustration.

When he checked on her later after dinner with the men, Sassy was fast asleep. Walking softly, he went into the living room and turned on the television. Sassy's commercial ran simultaneously on three major stations. "One way or the other," he muttered, "that woman's out to get me."

In the middle of the night he heard her fussing. "Aspirin," he reminded himself.

Wearing only the bottom half of his pajamas, he padded barefoot into the room. Moonlight spilled onto the bed, illuminating the outline of her figure. She was awake.

"Sassy, it's time for your aspirin." He leaned down to brush a lock of hair from her eye, his hand lingering on her cheek.

She gazed at him with eyes that he could drown in. They were deep blue in the reflected light. Her hair was a disheveled mass cascading down her shoulders. "Okay," she said. "I don't seem to be sleepy. Are you?"

His breath quickening, he looked at her long and hard. "Not anymore." He saw her grimace. "Is the pain bad?"

She arched her back. "It's more like a dull ache now, but my hip bothers me. I tried propping it on pillows, but nothing seems to work." She banged her fist on the mattress. "There's nothing I hate more than being a nuisance."

His mustache lifted as he smiled. His plans to run in and run out flew out the window. He eased himself onto the bed, letting her full weight rest on him. "There, is that better?"

"Much." The tension slowly eased from her side. Luke was being so generous when she knew he'd rather be doing something else. She searched her mind for a subject of interest to him. "Tell me about the cows. How often do they have calves?"

Luke rolled his eyes toward the ceiling. Of all the topics to pick. "They're in heat every twenty-one days. The bulls are ready and eager. If it takes, there's a calf. If not, they keep trying until they get it right."

She yawned. "Very interesting."

He grinned in spite of his uncomfortable predicament. She was finally falling asleep, while he was wide awake, thanks to her. He reached over to the night table for a glass of water. He brought it to her lips. "Right. Take the aspirin and let me get out of here."

Sassy's hand slid up his chest. "Stay with me a little while. Luke . . ."

Luke took a moment to study her. Memories of what he'd planned for this room warred with his good intentions. "Are you sure that's what you want?"

Sassy snuggled down, taking his hand with her, using it for a pillow. "Positive. You ask me a question," she mumbled. "I don't want to be alone."

He let his breath out slowly. The sensation of holding her was exquisite torture. Her foot touched his calf. His fingers tightened convulsively around her waist. If he weren't aware of Jerry's warning to let her have a good night's rest, his hand would have been on her breast not her waist, and he'd be easing the ache in his loins.

Luke said the first thing that popped into his mind. "All right. One question. Do you like modeling?"

He never heard the answer. Sassy mumbled and let out a deep sigh.

For better or worse, Luke thought, she was fast asleep, tangled in his arms, her derriere tucked into the curve of his body. Even if he wanted to move, which he didn't, he knew he was going to spend the night with her, holding her protectively.

Seven

When she awoke, Luke was gone. Only the warm indentation of where he'd slept let her know that he hadn't left her until early morning. During the night she'd felt his arms around her, his body supporting her aching side. He had murmured soothing words designed to make her sleep peacefully.

Thanks to Luke, she felt fine. She also realized she missed him in ways she didn't think possible. The bedroom, with its magical atmosphere, was getting to her. How nice it would be to live on the ranch with Luke, involved in this way of life, making a home with him.

In a short period of time, Luke had shown her what life might be like with him. She sensed his attraction to her, yet unless she was in trouble, he hid it behind a macho veneer.

Sassy heard his footsteps in the hall. He came into the room carrying a tray containing coffee, juice, a poached egg, and buttered toast. "What are you doing up?" he asked, deeply concerned for her welfare.

"Good morning to you, too, Mr. Grouch." She tossed her hair over her shoulder and mimicked his scowl.

Her playful spirit didn't cut ice with him. He put down the tray. "You're going to rest today." Sassy started to protest, but when he told her he'd stay with her, she lowered her gaze so he wouldn't see the mischievous gleam in her eyes. "On second thought, a day of rest won't hurt. Maybe later you can give me one of your magical massages?" It took so long for him to respond, Sassy winced for effect.

His voice sounded strangled. "All right. Eat up."

Sassy spent the day lounging on the porch. Luke had kept active with minor chores he was able to do while watching over her like a mother hen. He'd left her only to collect the eggs, clean out the stalls, pitch some hay, and let Sinbad and his stallion out into the corral.

Over a dinner of Dover sole made with sprigs of dill, and baked potatoes mashed with melted cheese, all prepared by Luke, he became an amateur psychologist, regaling her with stories of his stuntman experiences while prompting her to eat. If she slowed down, so did he. She successfully dragged out of him his best anecdotes, which resulted in peals of laughter or wide-eyed wonder at the tales.

"Does Jack Gregory really hate horses?" she asked, knowing the matinee idol had made his reputation on the back of a horse.

Luke waved his fork, noting Sassy had cleaned her plate. "With a passion. Most of the time the director shot him sitting on one of those mechanical jobs. I did his riding."

"But you're so much younger!" No one could deny Luke's virility. He filled the kitchen with his presence.

He had to stop himself from wanting to kiss her. "You'd be surprised how they can pad and age you," he said, thinking how different she was from the woman she'd portrayed in the television commercial. She was warm and real. The type of woman a man could fall in love with.

Not to be outdone, Sassy told him about a stunt she had pulled. "I wore a million dollars worth of diamonds with Cartier security men breathing down my neck. Out I came and smiled into the camera. It happened to be a commercial for toothpaste. The black gum I'd put over one of my teeth was a nice touch. The director didn't mind. The ad people even laughed. They were as slaphappy as we were after working twelve hours straight."

They spoke of everything except what was uppermost in their minds—their growing feelings for each other and what to do about them. Sassy curled up on the couch next to Luke, but by eleven P.M. her eyelids drooped. She stood up and winced, this time for real.

Luke's hands dropped to her waist, supporting her. "You're in pain?"

She nodded. "Only a little. Would you mind giving me another massage?"

The color drained from Luke's face, but he agreed. After she washed and changed into her gown, Luke repeated his healing massage on her bed.

Tingles of excitement replaced every other sensation. "Stay with me, Luke. For a little while."

Spending the day with her and spending the evening with her didn't rank equally in his mind. In the daytime he could find diversions. It had been all he could do to muster the self-control necessary to be with her on the couch and not make love to her.

Sassy was so tired, she couldn't see the expression on his face, nor could she know what her request cost him. Luke lay down next to her and cradled her in his arms. She fell asleep with her cheek on his shoulder. Luke brushed the hair from her forehead. He lightly kissed the corner of her eye. Sassy fit perfectly in his arms. Her scent aroused him.

Sometime after the witching hour, a welcome sleep overcame Luke, and he stopped wishing for what couldn't be.

"Sassy?"

"Hmmmm?"

"Your hand . . ."

Half asleep, she started to move it away from the hard, velvety ridge.

"No, don't," he mumbled, his voice heavy. Fumbling, he brought her hand back. "It feels good. . . . Ah . . . yes, just like that."

"I'm here for you, darling," she murmured, tasting her dream lover's lips. She arched her body. So many sensations. So many . . .

Her dream lover settled his mouth over her breast. His fingers glided over the curve of her hip, languorously stroking her inner thigh. "So moist, so ready for me." A soft sound of ecstasy escaped from her lips.

Sassy wrapped her arms around her dream lover's strong shoulders, shaping her hands on his taut muscles. He continued caressing her. Thinking ceased. She was lost in a current of honeyed, hot oblivion. Erotic images wove a web through her mind. Her mouth moved pliantly under his, lazily matching his arousing forays. Coils of heat gripped her lower body. Unconsciously she molded herself to its source, thrusting her hips closer, closer to her lover, her sorcerer, her sensual magician.

The urge to see him became overwhelming, the need to tell him how much she loved him overpowering. Struggling, she pushed away the veil of sleep clouding her mind.

Sassy's eyelids fluttered open. In her dazed state it took her another moment to orient herself. Sassy's breath puffed out of her. This wasn't a dream. Her nightgown was bunched up around her waist. She and Luke were locked in a compromising position. The dampness between her legs and at her breast wasn't a dream. She'd been responding to him like a wanton hussy. She hurriedly straightened her gown.

"Luke, wake up."

"What is it?" he grumbled, his speech slurred. "Don't you like it?"

She grabbed his chin, tilting up his head. "Luke, wake up."

His eyes blinked open angrily at the rude cessation of his own erotic dream. Glazed dark eyes stared into shocked blue ones. He sobered instantly, rolling onto his back. He cursed. Vividly. What game was she up to now, he wondered. If it had been up to him, he'd never have been in the room in the first place. Each time he came into it he was jinxed. What had started out to be the perfect setting in which to begin his marriage and create his children had become a torture chamber.

His body throbbed. He wanted her, and what surprised him even more was that he wanted more than her body. She had crept under his skin, molding herself to him like a hand tucked into his for safekeeping. He wanted to know her completely, to make love with her.

"What did you expect?" Luke asked, watching her eyes cloud. "I had my hands all over you last night. What do you think that does to a man, seeing a woman like you in his bed? Don't you dare blame me. I told you once I wasn't a good little boy. I'm a man, dammit."

Sassy's eyes misted. This wasn't the way it was supposed to happen. Not the first time. She was supposed to have candles and flowers and music and champagne, not be yelled at by an angry man who jumped to the wrong conclusions. She hugged the blanket up to her chin.

"Who said I blamed you?" she asked bitterly, wanting to spare herself another humiliating tongue-lashing. "The trouble with you, Luke Cassidy, is that you can't see a blasted thing in front of your stupid face except your dumb cows. You know something? I liked you better when you were asleep."

"What's that supposed to mean?" he asked, his attention riveted to her warm, sensual lips.

Her stomach churned nervously as she prepared to find the courage to say what was in her heart. In her sleep her body had chosen him. In her mind, she already knew she wanted him. Now, if she didn't lose her nerve, she was about to make one of the most important decisions of her life. If she did lose it, she'd be sorry forever.

Sassy hesitated briefly, her magnificent eyes begging him not to say or do a thing to mock her. She drew a deep breath. "It means, Luke Cassidy, that I want you to make love to me, only I want to be awake the first time."

He sat up, an awful suspicion going through his mind. He saw the flush of embarrassment on her face, confirming his fears. He was stunned at her admission. "Say that again," he said softly.

She lowered her lashes, unable to look at him. "I can't," she whispered achingly.

A muffled sound escaped him as he realized the true meaning of her offer. Out of all the men in the world, this gorgeous, sensitive, wonderfully brave girl had chosen him. His preconceived notions of her and her lifestyle vanished.

"Sassy," he said gently, already planning how he'd make love to her, "you are one constant surprise." And then because he was still amazed, he said, "What New York model is a virgin?"

Sassy shied away from his heated gaze, mistakenly concluding he thought her a complete dolt.

"Forget it," she muttered. "It was a dumb idea. I had this crazy notion that I wanted the first time to be perfect. In a perfect setting too. Like this room. There'd be flowers and music and champagne and . . ." She swallowed convulsively. Tears brimmed in her eyes. She tossed her head, turning away so he couldn't witness her mortification.

The cold protective wall Luke had built around his heart began to crumble. A surge of tenderness engulfed him. "And you think I'm the man and this is the perfect setting?" he asked softly, wondering how he could ever have misjudged her.

She swept her gaze around the room. It was cozy with Victorian elegance. Yet she knew her dreams of music and flowers and champagne meant nothing. Not really. Not without the right man.

"It was," she said in a whisper. "Until you spoiled it. The first time I came into this room and saw how romantic it was, I was filled with the feeling that all it needed was lovers to make it complete. It was as if I belonged here. Maybe that sounds crazy to you, Luke, but that's how I felt."

She clutched the sheet with nervous fingers and continued. "I knew that you'd decorated it with loving attention. When I asked you about it, you looked so sad. I knew you were hiding your feelings. It's what Peter said I've been doing, so I recognized it in you too." She lifted her shoulders. "It doesn't matter . . ."

"It matters very much," Luke said in a deep soothing voice. Putting his arm around her, he kissed away the tears filling her huge expressive eyes. "I think your idea is wonderful. You just took me by surprise, that's all. You have to admit that any woman who can turn on all the men in America just by crooking her little finger and then turns out to be a virgin is unique. Especially," he said thickly, his fingertips stroking her lovely face, "when you and I were already making love in our sleep. My body is a lot smarter than I am."

He tilted up her chin. "Sassy," he said, trying to find the words to put her at ease, "if it helps, I want you to know that from the first minute I saw you walk off the plane I was attracted to you. Frankly, I fought it for a lot of reasons. The night before last and then again last night when I gave you the massage, I recited everything I knew about cows in my head to keep from jumping out of my skin. Then when you asked me to stay with you"—he smiled—"well, you saw what happened."

Sassy lifted her hands, slowly tracing the outline of his lips. "Luke . . ."

His fingers were slowly working their way up her arms, unerringly drawing the sheet away. His gaze slid lower to the tops of her breasts. "Hmm?"

"Will you please kiss me? Now, when you're not angry anymore."

His chuckle was rich and compelling. "Whatever the lady wants," he said teasingly.

But there was nothing teasing about the way he kissed her. He crushed her to him, his mouth moving on hers in a soul-wrenching kiss. He made love to her with his mouth in a way that Sassy had never experienced before. He was bold and masculine and instructive. His tongue tangled with hers in a mating dance, plunging slowly in, then withdrawing, and when she strained closer, Luke picked up the tempo until Sassy felt as if the bed were swirling around her.

When he raised his head long moments later, they were both breathing hard. He kissed her eyelids. "Sassy, we're going to make love, and we're going to do it right, just the way you always dreamed it would be."

He left her for a moment to go into the other room. When he returned, he had a bottle of Chablis, two kitchen glasses, a small portable radio, and a yellow plastic rose.

He grinned. "It's the best I can do. The rose came with a present Maria received from Chester. She hadn't the heart to throw it out." He lit the candles on the vanity table, then poured wine into their glasses.

Sassy, her feet tucked under her, knelt on the bed, savoring every moment. She sipped the wine as Luke fiddled with the radio. "It's perfect."

If she weren't already in love with him, his boyish charm would have clinched it. Then she had an awful thought. "We can't. The men will be expecting breakfast."

"No, they won't," Luke assured her. "After dinner they headed up to the shacks on the line. They won't be back until Maria returns in time for dinner this evening. We're completely alone."

His eyes grew dark with passion. Sassy's breath caught in her chest. The little-boy Luke was no longer in the room. In his place was the passionate, caring man who would awaken her, then take her into full womanhood.

She raised her arms to help him as he lifted up her gown. Sassy glanced down at herself as he reverently touched her breasts, watching them reform in his hands. Her dreams could never match this reality, she thought.

Luke whisked his thumbs over her nipples. "So beautiful, so perfect." He lowered his head to take one nipple into his mouth. She was breathless and trembling as passion surged through her, touching every secret recess of her body. When she whimpered, he raised his head.

Luke let his gaze run over her supple figure. It was finely drawn and delicate. He wrapped a handful of sunshine-gold hair in his hand and drew her into his embrace. Kissing her, he shifted so that they lay facing each other.

In the candlelight her skin took on a sultry glow. She was exceedingly beautiful and, at the moment, vulnerable and innocent. "I'd give anything not to hurt you."

"Luke," she whispered, "you could never hurt me. I'm so glad it's you."

Her words of trust struck a deep chord within him. He crushed her to him, kissing her with all the pent-up emotion, all the raw unleashed power he'd been holding back. She was beautiful, alluring, and his.

She gasped as his hands began to ignite all the sensual places he'd touched in her dream. She wasn't shy, not after being held in his arms all night. His torso gleamed in the flickering candlelight. He was strong and gentle. "Teach me," she whispered, splaying her hands in his dark chest hair. "Teach me."

He groaned her name, pushing her back onto the mattress. His hands threaded through her hair. He kissed her passionately, touching her, lingering over her endlessly until she begged him to stop the sweet torture.

He heard the quickening of her breath, knew how ready she was for him. With one hand he cradled her head, while the other continued to arouse her.

She was being seduced by a sweetness more heady than any in her dreams, dissolving under the erotic onslaught of his mouth and his hands.

She wasn't aware of the tight rein he kept on his desire as he sought to pleasure her. He rained kisses all over her body until Sassy writhed under his touch. Overwhelmed by her feelings for him, she couldn't take her gaze from his handsome face. He saw all the trust in the world shining in her lovely turquoise eyes.

It was at that exact moment that Luke lost his heart.

Somehow, through divine providence, he'd been sent this marvelous creature to share his bed in this special room. He brought her to him, holding her fully against his aroused sex. His palms squeezed her buttocks. He buried his face in her fragrant hair. "Don't move," he said in a raspy voice, afraid of unleashing his own raging passion too soon. "I don't want to rush this. It's been a long time. Just let me hold you for a little while."

But Sassy ground her hips against him, shifting restlessly, inflaming him further. "Luke. Please . . ."

"All right, baby." He levered himself over her, parting her delicate thighs, lifting her hips to receive him. He was swollen and hard, urgent with need.

She gazed into his smoldering dark eyes, and she rejoiced in her decision to wait for the right man. She lifted her arms around his neck, curling her fingers into his hair. Slowly he bent his head to kiss her. He braced his weight on his elbows, introducing himself by degrees.

Sassy strained toward him, helping him, welcoming the full shaft of him. The sharp moment of pain receded quickly. Luke began to move inside her and Sassy rose to meet him. Her mouth on his was alive, seeking, devouring. Their tongues imitated the sex act. They were hungry for each other, wanting to give everything to the other.

Sassy had always hoped love would come to her this way. Luke was making it better than she'd ever imagined in all her dreams. Luke, his body joined to hers, held her and loved her as she exploded in a violent orgasm, crying out his name.

Knowing the joy of having satisfied her, Luke joined her in his own shattering climax. With their bodies fused, he took her to secret romantic places, blinding her with a thousand candles of light, and when finally the brightness dimmed, they were united in mind, in body, in spirit.

Eight

The morning sky was streaked with ribbons of gold. The candles on the vanity table had long since burned down. The bottle of wine was empty.

Sassy was snuggled next to Luke, who lay awake thinking after a brief but relaxing sleep. What happened between them wasn't like anything he'd experienced before. Out of all the women he had been with, even the woman he'd briefly been engaged to, Sassy was the only one who had given him her heart. He brushed the hair from her cheek, content to watch her while she slept. Then her eyes opened, and she smiled.

Luke ran the tip of his finger down her arm. "I didn't mean to wake you. How do you feel?"

"Hello," she said softly, gazing at him adoringly.

"How's the hip?" he asked, worried that their love-making might have been too much for her.

Sassy stretched languorously. "I feel better than I've felt in years," she confessed. "Nothing hurts. Do you want to get up?"

Pleased, he answered, "Not yet. There's one more thing I want to do." He eased himself off the bed, then dashed into the bathroom. He returned with her vial of wildflower perfume and a look of disappointment on his face. "Where're your leopard bikini panties?"

At her quizzical expression, he sent her a sheepish smile. "We all have our fantasies."

"You're serious?"

"Yup."

"They're in the bottom drawer, cowboy." As Luke foraged through the drawer like a man on a mission, Sassy, propped up on her elbow, laughed merrily as he held up a black silk teddy and a lacy white cutout bra. She giggled when he found his favorite pair of her panties and twirled them on his finger. "I'm going to take you up on your offer. I want you to model this for me."

"Now?"

"Right now," he said, meaningfully.

She slithered off the bed, naked, and in a playful mood. Luke lunged after her, kissing her bare bottom.

An hour later, he wore her panties on his thigh as a badge of merit. They'd made love again. She had met him with wild abandon, giving of herself passionately. Completing his fantasy, she'd modeled for him and now wore a black lace teddy cut high at the thighs and low at the neck.

"I don't know about you," he said, sighing contentedly, "but I'm getting too old for these marathon sessions." His fingers trailed an erotic path up her spine, while hers toyed with his mustache.

Sassy cocked an eyebrow at him. He had a satisfied grin on his face and could never pass for Methuselah. She interrupted her favorite pleasure, which at the moment was nibbling her way down his belly. "Youth will out. Maybe I'll find a younger lover," she teased. Luke was in his early thirties. She couldn't imagine ever wanting a lover more ardent than Luke.

"Don't even think about it," he said, pulling her face up to his. She was startled by what she saw in his eyes—passion and pain. Then his expression changed as he asked amiably, "What would you like to do today?"

She smiled impishly. "Take me for a ride on your horse. I don't hurt anymore, and besides, you promised to show me the ranch."

He groaned. "Haven't you had enough riding?"

"Oh," she said airily, "I think I could manage to stay on the horse if you're holding me. Unless you're too old and tired," she challenged with a wink.

"That's it. Off the bed. As long as there are no residual effects from your fall, and this morning proves there aren't, I'll grant your heart's desire and show you what a good sport I am. Let's go."

"Now?" He dragged her out of bed and into the bathroom. She shook her head as he turned the faucets in the tub on full force.

"Buster was in here last time. Today it's my turn."

"Luke Cassidy, did anyone ever tell you you're a voyeur?"

"Nope. Voyeurs watch. I'm going to participate."

"How?"

He leered at her. "Guess?"

The bath took longer than expected. Water sloshed onto the floor as Luke pulled her into his arms. She gasped as her eyes widened in shock. "Luke, do you know what you're doing?"

He growled against the soft curve of her hip, lifting her up and positioning her over him. "What do you think?"

She was too busy moaning in ecstasy to answer, but she thought he was marvelous.

An hour and a half later, after they'd had a quick breakfast and packed a picnic lunch, Luke saddled his stallion. With his arms protectively around her, they headed across the wide sage-strewn valley, into the foothills where piñon and aspen trees grew. He purposely steered away from where he knew Chester and the men would be working.

He wanted to be alone with her. He knew their time together would end soon, and he selfishly wanted to savor every moment. A sound off to the right alerted him.

"Uh oh, trouble. Hold on, there's a cow in labor. It's probably a breech."

"How can you tell?" Sassy asked, as they rode toward the animal.

"Experience." When they reached the animal, Luke helped Sassy down and went to the cow. He felt her distended belly, then rose. "She's not going to be able to deliver by herself. It's just as I suspected. The calf's in a breech position."

The cow thrashed fretfully. "Sassy, I'm going to hold her head down and tie her to that stump."

"What do you want me to do?"

"Get the rope for me. It's looped to the saddle."

She nodded and untied the rope from the saddle. Luke held the powerful animal's head. It wasn't easy but he managed to tie her so that she wouldn't hurt herself or him. Luke worked rapidly, explaining to Sassy that in a normal birth the calf's head was tucked between its legs.

"This little fella's supposed to come out feet and head first. He decided to be ornery."

Amazed and awed at the birth she was witnessing, Sassy watched Luke. He was sweating, concentrating on turning the calf in the birth canal. "Good, it's turning."

"Luke," Sassy cried, "I see it."

"You sure do," he said with a grunt, pulling the calf into position. "This baby is no lightweight either." With one more pull the calf slipped out of its mother. Luke broke the membrane surrounding the newborn to give it oxygen.

"Okay fella, it's mama's turn now." Luke attended to the cow, working to remove the placenta. When it was done, he sat back on his haunches for a moment.

He went to the saddlebag to find a towel. Spilling some water from the canteen onto it, he wiped the splattered blood from his arms and hands. "They'll be all right now." There was a broad smile on his face. "That's one more for the Circle C."

Sassy's pride in Luke changed the minute she saw him go to his saddlebag and return to the calf with a metal instrument in his hand. He crouched down near the baby, lifting one of its ears.

"What are you doing to him?" she protested.

Luke cast a look over his shoulder. "Notching his ear," he said, matter-of-factly.

"Don't do that," Sassy said sharply. "You'll hurt him. He's only a baby."

"This baby is my bread and butter," Luke said. He quickly notched the calf's ear. He caught the look on her face. "Sassy, if I don't do this, some other rancher will. The calf is my property. He'll be branded after the roundup. This is what I do. You model and act. I run a ranch."

She swallowed. Luke was reminding her of who and what she was. Without coming out and saying so, he also reminded her that this was his life. "Now I understand why the men eat such large breakfasts. They need the energy."

He watched the light go briefly out of her eyes. "That's what I tried to tell you. I'm glad you saw this. It's just a small part of what happens on a working ranch."

He didn't want her to have any illusions that his life was glamorous. Sassy was an idealist. He'd learned to be a pragmatist. Whatever they were sharing now would end.

Sassy swallowed, then said, "About the calf. . . . Is there any way you could keep him?"

"For what? A pet?"

"Would you?" He saw hope in her eyes. She didn't want this particular calf taken to market because she'd seen it being born, even though she knew the cattle were on his ranch for one purpose only. And it wasn't to make pets out of them.

He sat back on his haunches. Love was making him soft. "The best I can do is promise you he'll be raised here and used for breeding."

"How will you know which one Baby is?"

"Baby?"

"Actually, I think Cuddles is a better name."

Luke rolled his eyes. He marked the calf's ear with a dye. "You drive a hard bargain. Satisfied?"

Sassy leaped into his arms, throwing him flat on his back. She covered his face with kisses. Luke held his hands away from her, but the tender look in his eyes told her he was pleased he'd agreed.

"Up, woman," he said, catching the corner of her lip with a kiss. "You're smothering me. Come on, we're almost at the stream that leads to the pool where I swim. It's about fifty yards from here. We can wash there, then go on up to the pool. I want you to see it. If you like, we can stop for lunch there."

Thrilled with Luke's promise to keep the calf, Sassy said, "I like. That was quite an experience." She was still in awe of Luke's nonchalant acceptance of how he'd saved the cow and her calf. They mounted the horse and started off. "How many cattle do you have?"

"We keep approximately twenty cows for each bull to service . . . about two thousand in all."

"Sounds to me as if the bulls have all the fun and the cows have all the work."

"Spoken like a woman." They rode along in silence for a few minutes. Then Luke said, "Look at these mountains. They contain gold and silver."

"But I don't see any mining equipment."

"If the geologists feel it's worth reopening the mines, then they'll make an offer."

"What does that depend on?"

"Although this is desert country, there's a heck of a lot of water in these mountains. Pumping it out adds to the cost of production. At today's labor costs and with market fluctuations, it's not always financially expedient to reopen an old mine. There will be some representatives coming to look the place over." He didn't tell her the men were due tomorrow and he'd be riding out to meet them.

"Imagine," she said with a laugh. "I could be riding with King Midas and not know it."

"In the meantime you're riding with a dirty cowboy. There's the stream up ahead."

She made a face at him and he laughed. It struck him that he hadn't laughed so much or felt so relaxed in years. Sassy was good company, in every way. He made a mental note to call Peter and thank him.

After they washed in the stream, Sassy lay near a tree, her face raised to the late morning sun. She knew she'd never forget watching Luke with the cow as long as she lived. She felt very proud for the small part she'd played in helping him.

"Come on, lazybones. I want to show you something." He helped her up. Leaving the stallion ground-tied, they walked to a stand of apple trees. They were laden with little green apples. "Here, try one. They're small, but good."

She did, tentatively at first, then with appreciation. "Delicious."

He smiled at her. "Wait a minute. You've got juice on your chin. No, don't," he said, halting her hand. "I've got a much better idea."

She was acutely aware of his masculine scent as he drew her to him for a long, leisurely kiss. She surfaced on a sigh. "Luke, this is such a perfect day."

His eyes shining, he said simply, "I meant it to be."

She shook one of the low-hanging branches. "Let's take some apples back with us. I'll bake you an apple pie."

The image of her baking in his kitchen stirred his imagination. He quickly squelched the domestic pictures of Sassy as mistress of his house. He would take what he could for the short period of time that he was allowed. She'd be leaving soon to go on to a film career. "Apple pie's my favorite," he said, helping to pick more fruit.

"Then we'll pick as many as you want," she said, moving with unconscious grace. She was enormously pleased to be able to do something nice for Luke.

There was a stark beauty to the high desert country. Though she'd made many trips to the Metropolitan Museum of Art and other museums throughout the world to study costuming, nothing compared with the colors and hues of nature. As she gazed around her at both the vibrant mountain greenery and the muted tones of the desert shrubbery, she wished more than ever that she'd brought a sketch pad with her.

"These colors are absolutely magnificent. If it's all

right with you, I'd like to go into town tomorrow to buy a sketch pad."

"Do you draw?" He lifted her up on the horse.

"Design clothes," she corrected. "Someday when I'm put out to pasture as a model, I'd like to design for a living." She didn't tell him she wished it would happen for her sooner rather than later.

"What about your movie career? Aren't you excited about it?"

"My mother is more excited than I am. I guess I'm the only woman in America not eager to see herself up on the screen."

Sassy sounded so unconvinced, Luke was certain she was afraid her acting ability wouldn't measure up.

"You'll be a big hit. Believe me, I can tell." Now it was he who sounded morose. Sassy rested her head on his shoulder, smiling when he leaned over to kiss the tip of her nose. "You can grow on a man, do you know that?"

She gave him a beguiling smile. "Thank you kind, sir. I aim to please."

His face grew solemn. He blurted out the truth before he could stop himself. "Don't. I'd hate to think of you pleasing another man."

She twisted around, her eyes glittering, her face flushed. "Tell me," she said, matching Luke's seriousness, "do you really think I'd do with anyone else what we do together? Because if you do, you can let me off right here, Luke Cassidy."

He stopped the horse, not to let her off, but to kiss away the hurt in her eyes. Jealousy was foreign to him, but since meeting Sassy he'd been filled with it. He knew she'd be leaving soon, which he hated but accepted.

"I'm sorry, sweet. I guess I'm missing you already. I had no right to say that to you."

She glumly agreed. "Luke, what are we going to do?"

He hugged her, steeling himself for the day he'd have to put her on a plane for California.

He put a positive note in his voice. "We're going to enjoy the present and not think about anything but us today."

The sun dimmed for Sassy. There was harsh reality in the words he'd spoken. He couldn't know how his words pierced her heart.

He hadn't mentioned one word about love or their future. And why should he? He'd made it plain right from the beginning that they were traveling on different paths.

"You're right, Luke," she said, cloaking her disappointment with a carefree tone. "We'll live for today."

She'd passed her first demanding acting lesson.

Nine

Feathery tufts of cirrus clouds wisped across a sky painted a brilliant shade of blue. The temperature was in the low eighties. The crystal clear pool lay nestled in a cove fed by a rushing waterfall that spilled over a rocky outcrop. It was as if they'd stepped back to another century, alone and protected in the small valley by sentinels of pines and aspens and soaring mountain peaks. Here the land was richer, softer, greener. It smelled of moist flowers and moss.

Sassy lay with her head resting on Luke's chest, listening to the steady thrum of his heart. She was determined not to allow anything to mar their day together. She'd fallen in love, and she would take the consequences. Was it selfish of her to want more? Luke's feelings for her, she knew, weren't as intense as hers for him. He belonged on the ranch, while she wasn't certain where she belonged, only that it wasn't in New York or Los Angeles or Rome or Paris or any of the other fast-paced cities where she'd lived and worked.

She cuddled closer to Luke, allowing herself the luxury of pretending. How strange, she thought, that a man whose lifestyle was so totally different from hers would be the one to show her what it means to feel cherished, even for a little while. When he looked into her eyes and told her he wanted her, she felt beautiful in a way no camera could detect. It was as if every cell in her body had been rearranged to match his perfectly.

If she could, she'd freeze time and stay with Luke in the sequestered glen forever. With the birds twittering in the trees, with the rabbits and chipmunks and squirrels scurrying past them, with the trees to hide them, with the brush of the wind in her hair and the warmth of the sun on the mountains.

And with Luke to hold her and love her at night.

Luke, who was strong and good and unbelievably kind and gentle. She smiled. He'd hate to be called gentle, but that's exactly what he was.

"Penny for your thoughts?" Luke trailed a possessive hand down her thigh. He skimmed his gaze over her face. How could he let her go when he'd just found her?

I was thinking that I love you. "My thoughts are priceless. You'll have to go higher. Penny for yours?"

Easy, he thought. *I was thinking that I love you.* "Not fair. I asked first." He wanted to make love to her, there in the place where no woman had ever been with him. He would lay her down on the ground with only the aspens as a bower. And he would gaze at her naked body as the rays of light sundanced on her skin.

Sassy twirled a purple flower under her nose. "It's too bad most people think the desert is colorless. They miss the extraordinary blessing God has paid the earth. Their loss."

He couldn't stop his lips from curving. He was enormously pleased with her reaction to the section of the ranch he'd shown her. Most city girls would have looked at the vast open spaces and seen just that. Not Sassy.

"Mmmm. Most people only see tans and browns and sparseness. You're very rare, do you know that?"

"Of course," she said, tugging at his mustache.

He had been prepared for Sassy to make a complimentary gesture, but he hadn't been prepared for all the questions she peppered him with. She kept him mentally on his toes as he strove to remember the names of the plants that grow at various elevations. Sassy, he'd learned, saw beauty and color in every rock, every plant and shrub.

"Some people collect stamps. Some collect jewels. I prowl museums. The Metropolitan Museum of Art regularly displays collections of costumes," she said enthusiastically, chattering on about the topic that interested her most—designing. "There are other places, of course. Anyway, all the best designers in the world copy nature's palette. For example, look at the sky. What do you see?"

"Blue."

"Oh, you!" She laughed, tugging again on his mustache. "Well, don't you dare tell me those clouds are white," she said pertly.

"They are," he said, getting the last word.

A comfortable silence settled between them. His fingers drifted sensually across her cheek. He lifted his thumb, tracing it along the tip of her nose to her mouth where he dipped it into the sweet, seductive line separating her lips.

"Where do you show your collection?" he asked after a while.

A flock of bright yellow birds flew overhead. Sassy's gaze followed the lead bird until the formation was out of view. She instantly imagined the color on a spring suit with blue accents.

Bringing her attention back, she answered, "I haven't shown my line for the simple reason there's nothing but sketches to show." It was hard to think now that Luke had begun to stroke her thigh. "My problem is time," she said after a while. "That and the fact that I need to hire a cutter and a seamstress."

Luke was tempted to tell Sassy about Maria's dexterity with a sewing machine. But what good would it do? Even if Sassy were to give up modeling and acting, her interests were better served in a large city. Famous fashion designers weren't known to hide out in small desert towns. Sassy, he realized, was becoming very important to him, which would make it harder for him to deal with her leaving. In the meantime he didn't want to think, he only wanted to feel. He became intensely aware of the scent of her perfume, the lilt of her voice.

He played with the golden strands of her hair, sifting them through his fingers, watching as it caught the light. Her long lashes swept up, framing eyes the shade of a blue-green sea. She looked very pretty and very, very desirable. "I haven't been this lazy in years."

"Mmmm, me either," she said. She could smell the water. If she could work up the energy, she decided, she'd unpack the saddle bag. Then she'd change into her bathing suit and go for a swim. "Listen to the music of the water, Luke. It's playing a song."

"I'd rather listen to you," he said, tipping her chin up to give her one of his melting smiles.

"How is it that you've never married, Luke?"

The mood was shattered. Luke's face tightened for a moment. He fixed his sights on a bird pulling a worm from the dampened earth near the edge of the water. "A long time ago someone convinced me that I'm a confirmed bachelor."

"Nonsense," Sassy retorted, hearing the cynicism in his tone and hating the person who helped put it there. Luke was too warm a man, too loving by nature to spend his life alone. She gestured with the flower she'd picked. "Men like you are meant to be married."

Her statement made his dark eyebrows shoot up.

"What exactly do you mean by that, Miss Worldly Wise?" he asked, amused.

"You're making fun of me when I'm being serious," Sassy chastised, resolving to say what was on her mind while she had his complete attention and before she lost her nerve.

"Fire away, then," he said, resigned. "I have an idea you will anyway."

"For one thing, your home is too big."

"My house?" he asked, totally surprised. "What does my house have to do with it?"

Sassy immediately sat up, gesturing with her hands as she explained. "You call it a house. I referred to it as a home. There's a big difference, you know."

"So?"

"So which is the only room you bothered to decorate?" she asked candidly. "It may be a bachelor's house now, but it didn't start out that way in your mind. If you're honest with yourself, you'll admit it. Hear me out before you interrupt," she said, aware he wasn't pleased.

"Hurry up though. This conversation is getting us nowhere."

"That's because you're the center of attention. You don't even like talking about the book you wrote or your experiences as a stuntman. You buried the past so deeply, you haven't dealt with it."

He ran his fingers through his hair. A muscle flickered slightly in his cheek. It seemed they were both good at burying their pasts. "Your point?"

"My point is," she said, noting the guarded expression in his eyes, "that your house should be a home. It's ideal for a large family. A family of your sons and daughters, growing like sprites before your eyes. Where you can teach them values, like love and commitment and, yes, the value of hard work too. This ranch is perfect for you. Imagine being able to come to a heavenly spot like this for a picnic and a swim. You wouldn't need to drive through a crowded city or get mugged on the corner."

"And that's why you think I should have married?" he asked. "Because of a swimming hole and acreage?" Her animated face was full of passion and fire. He'd witnessed the same fire in her eyes earlier when he'd held her in his arms.

"If that's all you heard of what I said, it's too bad." With a sigh she let the flower in her hand slip from her fingers. Luke had adroitly backed her into the corner of her argument. If she pressed her point that he should have married, it lessened the value of their lovemaking, labelling it an interlude and nothing more. If she spoke the absolute truth and told him she was grateful he hadn't married, but thought he now should be, it would sound as if she were tricking him into asking her to marry him.

"I suppose it is a pretty lame reason after all," she said, reconsidering.

Luke saw the mutinous expression on her face. In a few short days his life had been thrown into a topsy-turvy array of emotions by this lovely creature. From an acute case of lust, he'd advanced to a feeling of sympathy and concern for her when she'd fallen from Sinbad, only to have that sympathy graduate into a deep awareness that Sassy meant so much to him now, he didn't want to face the thought of her leaving.

She'd unlocked feelings he'd buried for years and made him question his status as a bachelor. And she'd given him the greatest gift a woman could give. Herself. His precious Sassy truly believed in love ever after.

He wasn't going to burst her bubble with the truth. The fact that he was in love with her disturbed him greatly. Their lifestyles could never mesh. He was, in short, caught between the devil and the deep blue sea, with him being the devil and Sassy's luminous turquoise eyes the sea.

"Assuming I were to marry," Luke said, keeping his voice purposefully neutral, "what kind of a woman would you suggest I look for?" He turned the full force of his midnight gaze on her and waited.

Sassy's heart hammered in her chest. "Not the woman who made you a cynic, that's for sure," she blurted out, wishing she could apply for the role.

"You think I'm a cynic?" he asked, genuinely puzzled that after all the times they'd made love, she could think that.

"Tell me about her."

"Who?"

She felt him stiffen, but she'd started and she wasn't going to stop. "The woman who turned you into a cynic."

In another time he might have smiled and asked Sassy to marry him right then. "There's nothing to tell. It was over a long time ago."

"If it was over a long time ago, why can't you talk about it?" Sassy asked.

"All right. A long time ago I was engaged to an actress who was very ambitious. We'd worked on a couple of movies together. After I was injured we agreed to call it off. End of story."

End of story. A wave of sadness overcame her as she tried to fathom why his former fiancée would have rebuffed him when he'd needed her most. "How were you injured?"

He shifted his shoulders. "A fuse triggering a line of powder charges went off prematurely. I hadn't gotten into a safe position yet when they blew. If it weren't for Peter visiting the set that day, I might not be here. I owe him a lot. Certainly I wouldn't be walking, much less riding if it weren't for him. We've been friends ever since. He usually visits here twice a year. Anyway, after the doctors discharged me from the hospital, I bought this place."

He'd masked the horrible accident in perfunctory terms, which she knew was far from the truth. Sassy's heart ached for the younger Luke whose career had ended so drastically. She admired him greatly. He'd fought his way back and had gone forward with his life.

"And Chester came with you," she said, her voice filled with pride in Luke's accomplishments. "He told me you two worked together in the movies."

Luke rubbed his cheek against her hair. "Maria too. Her career had taken a nosedive, so when Chester and I came here, she volunteered to be the cook. Sometimes I get the sneaking suspicion she didn't want to let Chester out of her sight."

Sassy's eyes widened. "You mean Maria and Chester are having an affair?"

Luke chuckled. He gave Sassy's shoulder a quick squeeze. "Chester would never admit it, but when Maria returns, you'll notice he hangs around her a lot. Playing cupid for them is the least I can do. One of these days that old dog is going to wise up and marry her."

Sassy wondered when the "young pup" who was

capable of making such fiercely tender love to her would wise up and want to get married, too, but she said nothing.

She'd seen with her own eyes the intense loyalty he evoked in the people who worked for him.

"Where's your family, Luke?"

He smiled at her. Even now, talking companionably about their pasts, he wanted her. He cleared his mind. "My family is spread out to the four winds. I've got a sister, Pam, who's married to a man named Jerry Hickson. He's a captain in the Air Force and stationed in Germany. No children yet, much to my parents' disappointment.

"Dad's a veterinarian. He recently retired. They bought a bus, had it fixed up so they could use it as a mobile home, and off they went while they were still young enough to enjoy traveling. Last I heard from them, they were in the Old City of Quebec, practicing their French. They were around for the bad times. They're good people. We all try to get together at Christmas. So far Jerry's been able to wangle it. What about you?"

Sassy swallowed hard, envying his family ties. She had none to match. No stories to share. She dipped her head. "You already know about me."

Luke lifted a hand to draw her face up. Her eyes were sad. It was obvious to him that he was treading on touchy ground.

"Where's your father? You spoke about your mother being your manager."

For a full minute she was silent, and he thought she wasn't going to respond. When she did, her voice was cold and remote. There wasn't a trace of the warm Sassy he knew.

"My father left home one day when I was little. He never came back. As you say, 'End of story.' "

Astounded, Luke said, "But surely he kept in contact with you while you were growing up?"

Reminded of all the times she held her father's picture in her hand, talking to it, hoping that he'd call, she bit her inner lip. She withdrew into a place Luke couldn't reach.

"No. Mother gave me birthday and Christmas presents that were supposedly from him. She made up stories why he had to be away. She even went so far as to write letters. One day I was searching in her closet for one of her handbags to play with. On the top shelf I found my presents. My birthday was the next day, and I was excited. There was a letter. I opened it. It was the final divorce decree. The grounds were desertion. After that, there was no more need to pretend."

Sassy shuddered, and Luke instinctively held her closer. "It was my career that got in the way. Mother started me on a modeling career when I was two. The money was good. I worked constantly. My father, well . . . he resented it when I made more money than he did. It took me a long time to understand that my father was a man who craved attention."

Luke's blood boiled. He instantly hated the man and resented her mother's misguided judgment in letting Sassy believe a cruel lie. Both parents had used her. Sassy's father had gotten attention all right. Thanks to him, Sassy carried guilt around and still couldn't wipe his perfidious action from her mind. Ending a marriage was one thing, but leaving a child was unforgivable, Luke thought.

He deliberately drew Sassy's chin up, forcing her to meet his eyes. She was stiff and withdrawn, caught in the cold catacomb of her memories. He bit back an oath, speaking calmly for her sake. "Honey, whatever happened between your parents should have been their problem to work out, not yours. Surely you know now that you were the innocent victim?"

She brushed at an insect near her leg. "Intellectually, yes. All children are victims in a divorce. From a practical standpoint, there's nothing I can do, except what I'm doing now."

"Which is?"

"Coping. Sorry, that's the wrong term. A lot of women would envy me. No, I'm trying to come up with a way my mother and I can part on good terms, so that she can continue as a manager for someone else. I will not leave her high and dry. Regardless of anything else, she's always been there for me, and I love her. I won't let her down. I couldn't live with myself if I did."

His heart melted. She was fiercely protective of her mother. He smoothed her heavy golden hair away from her forehead. Taking her face in his hands, he said, "Sassy, your father was a weakling. Instead of working out an arrangement to shoulder his responsibility, he copped out. That's his loss. Do you know what's happened to him?"

Her eyes clouded. She tossed her head defiantly. "He's dead. Dead. He died poor and alone, in Hawaii of all places. A luxury island. My father was a charmer who simply ran out of charm." Her lower lip trembled. Luke let her speak, knowing she needed to get it all out. "We had unfinished business, and he died."

Luke thought it was nothing more than the man deserved, but held his tongue. "There's the future. If you were doing what you truly want to do, designing clothes and marketing them, Peter would never have sent you to me."

"Are you sorry?" she whispered, lifting her gaze to his.

He smiled. "Have I been acting sorry?"

"Be serious."

"I am serious. Whatever else might be said about our mutual friend Peter, you have to give him credit for introducing us."

For a while Sassy and Luke sat holding each other, clinging to all the newly learned facts they'd exchanged. Telling Luke about her father had been a catharsis for her. In turn he had given her much to think about.

"Now, young lady," he said finally, lightening the mood, "I don't know about you, but I'm going swimming."

She changed her clothes, putting on the black bathing suit Beth had given her. Luke whistled when he saw her in it. It consisted of two crisscross bands of black lycra material that covered her in the strategic places. "Did you ever model this suit?"

"No, a friend gave it to me. She said it would get me a cowboy. Was she right?" Sassy asked, her voice husky.

His gaze ran slowly down her body. He already felt the familiar tightening in his loins. "Your friend isn't much of a mind reader. You're a knockout in anything you wear."

It was more than her outward appearance, Luke knew. Sassy had that rare inner glow that only enhanced her surface beauty. He wondered how he'd ever be able to say good-bye to her. When she described a home, he'd seen the yearning in her eyes. Now that he knew about her father, he understood Sassy better. She had a strong sense of responsibility and loyalty. For a person who had been reared by a single parent and had been in the limelight all her life, her two feet were planted solidly on the ground. He reluctantly acknowledged that Mrs. Shaw had done a good job raising Sassy.

It was time to put their relationship back in perspective. Before he'd let himself cautiously begin to hope for the future, he had to make certain the lure of the silver screen wasn't seeded in her, awaiting the right combination of circumstances to bloom. He knew it was a heady experience to be in the movies, regardless of the fact that Sassy thought she'd be immune. Anything could happen once she got back out there in the world.

She could also meet other men. . . .

He halted, not far from the pool. "See here," he began in a tone so serious, it drew Sassy's head up sharply.

"Luke," she said, taken aback by the formidable look on his face, "what is it?"

He cleared his throat. "I think I should give you the benefit of my experience."

"Your experience?" she asked, earning a positive nod. Totally confused, both by his manner and his sudden mood change, Sassy stared at the handsome, dynamic man, who looked as if he wanted to throttle an unseen intruder.

"You may find," he advised seriously, "that when you arrive on the movie set, there will be people— men—who will try to take advantage of you."

"Advantage of me?" She became suspicious of his erect posture, the savage line of his lips, the rebellious tug of his mustache. Luke looked ready to explode. She pressed her lips together, trying to keep a straight face.

In his mind's eye, he saw her writhing naked in his arms, responding to his most intimate caresses. "Yes," he said with a scowl. "Unscrupulous men who wish to make a conquest of you because of your beauty, your charm, your sensual loveliness, your—." A ripple of laughter rumbled out of her lips. She slapped her hand over her mouth. "Why are you laughing?" he asked.

Her eyes twinkling, Sassy flung her arms around Luke's neck. "I just wanted to be sure you're warning me for my own good."

"Why else would I be saying this?" he asked.

She caught her breath. Luke loved her. He was petrified to admit it. Loving him the way she did, she'd wait until he found the words. In the meantime she'd settle for seeing desire written all over his glowering, gorgeous, grumpy, jealous face.

"Tell me, cowboy, these unscrupulous men you're referring to—were you by chance one of them when you were working in the movies?"

"Certainly not," he said, knowing full well he hadn't been a saint, which made him worry more.

She coyly lowered her lashes, then dazzled him with a teasing smile. "Then are you now? Taking advantage of me for my—how did you put it?—my charm, my beauty, my sensual loveliness?"

"Sassy," he said sternly, dragging her arms away from his neck to scold her, "I'm telling you this for your own good. The least you can do is appreciate it."

"Oh," she said with a gasp smothering a smile. "I do appreciate it."

He shook her wrist. "You don't act it. Now listen carefully."

Sassy, who was well versed in knowing how to protect herself, listened and watched in fascination as Luke's face became redder and redder. He treated her to a discourse on self-protection, even explaining a few techniques in martial arts. Unable to disguise the madcap mood he'd put her in, she fell apart, laughing hysterically.

Luke glared at her. He was trying to save her, but he had the urge to shake her until her teeth jarred loose. "Sassy, you are an impertinent, impudent, saucy, fresh-mouthed, smart-alecky woman. I think it's time you went for a swim."

Sassy squealed, taking a furtive step backward. Luke moved with pantherlike grace, scooping her up effortlessly in his arms. He threw her over his shoulder, carrying her like a sack of potatoes. Her head bobbed, her hair hung down.

"Oh, no you don't," she said, giggling, her arms

and legs flying. Certain he meant only to tease her, she good-naturedly went along with the game, pounding her fists on his back. Luke grunted and kept walking.

Birds twittered in the trees as if they enjoyed having front row seats to watch the dark-haired man and the blond-haired beauty engage in crazy shenanigans.

Luke took four giant steps into the water. "You wouldn't dare?" Sassy yelped.

Ignoring her protests completely, Luke lifted a laughing Sassy high in the air, then dropped her with a splash.

She came up sputtering and pushing long strands of hair out of her eyes and mouth. With a devilish smirk, Luke tucked his arm around her waist, pulling her out of the water and out of her suit as if he were Houdini.

"Now what are you doing?" she asked.

"Making it easier for you to swim." His tone was silky smooth.

"You devil," she burst out. He grinned, working his clothes off just as rapidly.

Sassy suspected what was coming next. Her pulse speeded up. His hand slipped beneath the water. A wild sweep of pleasure exploded inside her as Luke began to slowly stroke her sleek skin. "Luke," she said, gasping, "you wouldn't."

He did.

Thoroughly. Expertly. Masterfully.

When their passion was sated, he carried her back to the blanket.

Leaning over her, he said, "Do you know how much I wanted to barge into the bathroom when you were taking your bath?"

Pleasure filled her. She hadn't known the attraction had started for him then too. Sassy closed her eyes, drawing in the memory of what had just happened in the pool. Luke made her world come alive. Luke. Luke's scent. Luke's strength.

He watched her face, then needing her again with a violence he hadn't dreamed possible, he lowered his head to her breast and turned her universe into a sensual paradise.

"How do you feel?" he asked, quite a while later.

She gazed into his stormy eyes, humbled by her ability to make this proud man tremble with desire.

"I feel," she whispered, her voice choking with emotion, "I feel . . . complete."

By the time they returned home, Maria would be there, Luke was sure. At dinner time the men would pile into the house. Everything would return to normal.

Both of them agreed they'd rather remain in their magical sanctuary, where they were the only two people who existed.

Ten

As expected Maria greeted them at the door when they returned. Her single, thick jet-colored braid worn down her back was as dark as Sassy's was golden. She was in her early forties, Sassy judged, and she carried her Indian and Spanish heritage proudly. Lively brown eyes warmly appraised Sassy. She held out her hand.

"I've seen you on television and on the covers of magazines. Chester tells me you fell from Sinbad. I'm glad there were no harmful effects."

"Luke took good care of me," Sassy answered, hearing Maria's voice soften when she mentioned Chester's name. Sassy couldn't help wondering whether Maria could tell from their faces that she and Luke were lovers.

Maria took the bag of apples from Sassy and brought the fruit to the kitchen sink to wash it. Sassy followed. "You had a phone call from your mother, Sassy."

Sassy felt the chill of the outside world closing in on her. Her gaze flew to Luke's. He looked as grim as she felt.

"Use the phone in the den. You'll have more privacy."

Phyllis Shaw came straight to the point. "Sassy, you knew when you left home that Jamie Rudolpho's people were scouting for a shoot location on a ranch. My helping them by suggesting Cassidy's ranch seemed like a natural solution. I thought you'd be excited and pleased."

She wasn't. She wouldn't allow her relationship with Luke to be put on a business basis. "Mother, I'll go anywhere else."

"Sassy, it's probably too late. Jamie Rudolpho loves my idea. He personally asked me to follow up on it. I don't have to tell you he's the hottest name in fashion. He believes in you. This campaign is vital for your career. The timing is perfect. The ads will open doors. Don't you realize the publicity value? Jamie benefits from the tie-in to the movie. You benefit by finally having your name on a line of clothing. Isn't that what you've always wanted?"

"My own, not someone else's." A professional, Sassy knew her mother was right about her career advice. "Even if I wanted to, it's an imposition," she argued. "I won't put Luke in that position."

"In what position?"

At the sound of Luke's voice Sassy turned. Her

shoulders drooped. Covering the receiver, she drew a long, shuddering breath, repeating the nature of her mother's phone call. Tears glittered on her lashes. "Naturally, I told her no. I'll be leaving sooner than I expected."

"Let me speak with her," Luke said with quiet firmness.

Sassy shook her head. "It's my business. I'll work it out."

Luke took the phone from her. Several minutes passed with Sassy growing more agitated as she listened to Luke interject a yes or no with little explanation.

"Your mother's a sensible woman," Luke said, when the call ended. "The two of us ought to get on well." His hands were on her face, smoothing away the worry lines. "Now what do you say we go back into the kitchen, break out the bubbly, and make a toast?"

Jumping up from the chair, Sassy pushed Luke's hands away and began pacing the floor. Luke had lost his mind. He was insane. Nuts! If he agreed to this nonsense and allowed the shoot to be filmed at his ranch, the place would be overrun with all sorts of people, demanding things he'd hate. No, she decided. She'd leave before she'd allow that to happen to him. As for drinking a toast with Luke, there was nothing she felt less like doing than celebrating her imminent departure.

"A toast? What do we have to toast?" she asked, throwing her arms out wide.

He grinned unrepentantly. "Can you think of a

better man to play an authentic American cowboy? You do agree I can perform some pretty wild stunts on a horse, don't you?"

Blushing furiously, she nodded. Luke had made love to her while galloping across the desert. Stunned, she'd clung to him, rocketing from revelation to rapture.

He wanted to meet her mother and judge his competition for himself. Any woman who set her sights on stardom for her client wasn't about to step aside and see her dreams evaporate, particularly when it involved her own daughter. In the meantime, the kindest thing he could do for Sassy was not to complicate her life.

"Speaking of horses," Sassy said later at dinner, drawing Luke back into the stream of conversation around the table, "what happened with Sinbad was my fault. I wasn't experienced enough to know what to do when the snake spooked him, so I've decided to give it another shot tomorrow."

The fork in Luke's hand stilled. He refused to consider the possibility she might be thrown again. "No, you're not riding Sinbad tomorrow."

At his flat dismissal, Sassy's chin came up defiantly. He'd deliberately refused her without a reason. The conversation ceased. All heads turned toward Sassy to see how she'd handle him.

Her face heated with embarrassment. "You said yourself that everyone falls. Isn't that right, boys?" She had the brief satisfaction of hearing a chorus of agreement from the men. "You even said the best cure when a person falls is to get right back on again."

"In your case I was wrong."

In disbelief she watched him lift his fork and ask Meriman to pass the biscuits. "Does that mean if I can't ride like Annie Oakley the first time on a horse, it's all over? I never heard anything so dumb in my life. You're going to have to do better than that," she demanded. Their audience was silent.

Luke scraped the chair out from under him, tossing down his napkin on his plate. "Am I?"

In a like action Sassy sprang to her feet too. She planted herself in front of him, her hands on her waist. Throwing her shoulders back, she gave him a hard, assessing look, which clearly said she intended to have her way. If Luke Cassidy was going anywhere, he'd have to contend with her first.

Temper born of worry edged Luke's voice. He put his hands on her shoulders. "Sassy, you're not riding Sinbad. I don't want to be responsible for you falling and hurting yourself again." That much he could tell her and not feel like a louse.

She breathed a sigh of relief. "Is that all?" She smiled confidently, relaxing her stance. She put her hands on his chest. "You're not responsible—"

"And," he continued, wishing they didn't have an audience, "I refuse to be responsible for you not getting to the coast in time to start your movie."

Sassy bristled. She should have known. He'd warned her fair and square. Permanence and commitment weren't words in his vocabulary, but she hadn't expected to be reminded so bluntly, not after everything they'd shared. Her romantic notion that Luke might be falling in love with her died, and with it a little piece of her heart. Luke had made it abundantly clear in front of witnesses that his chief worry was getting her back on the plane and out of his life in one piece. Damn him. If she'd stayed in the room with him one second longer, she'd explode.

She forced her voice to be calm, even giving it a note of sweet appreciation for his concern over her welfare. She could not, however, do anything about her eyes. They flamed with indignation. Luke noted it and accepted it. He'd deal with her later when they were alone.

Her hands came down to her sides. She allowed her fingers to relax. She called on her acting talent to stem the flow of threatening tears. "You're perfectly right, Luke. Thank you for suggesting that I might be jeopardizing my career." She smiled brightly at the cowboys but avoided looking at Maria. Women couldn't fool women. "As long as we're on the subject of my career, gentlemen, I need my beauty sleep. So if you'll excuse me, it's been a long, enlightening day."

Luke dug his hands into his back pockets as he watched her leave the room. Sassy had snuck past his defenses, leaving him as vulnerable as a lovesick teenager. If they had a chance, and he prayed they did, it would have to be after Sassy experienced the reality of being an actress.

If she ever came back to visit, he'd teach her anything she wanted to know. Sinbad was too much horse for her. He'd buy a gentle mare who was a little deaf. That way the horse couldn't hear a rattler. Or maybe he'd just keep her by his side where he could watch out for her safety.

Buster trotted down the hall with Sassy, slipping past her into the bathroom to flop onto the mat near the bathtub. She turned on the tap to fill the tub and leaned against the bathroom door, trembling. The enormity of Luke's statement sank in further. She ran her hand through her hair. What a dope she'd been. What a colossal dope. She'd given Luke her most precious gift, and he'd flung it back in her face.

Thanks to her mother she was stuck. She'd do Jamie Rudolpho's layout, pose on the horse with Luke, then leave with whatever dignity she had left.

She'd do the polite thing. She'd send him a thank you note and a gift. No, she thought, hitting on a better idea. It might be tacky, but Luke was going to get her first autographed studio picture. She'd sign it "You were right."

She let the blessed relief of tears come. The thing was, she thought, he *wasn't* right. They were so good together. Twisting her heavy hair on top of her head with a few deft turns, she secured it in place with two barrettes. Before stepping into the tub, she turned up the volume of the radio, blasting away her ability to think.

The steamy mist in the room condensed on the tiles, then dripped down the walls. Sitting up in the water, Sassy bent her knees. Bypassing the washcloth she soaped the sponge. With a few vicious strokes she scrubbed her long legs. Leaning forward, she rested her head on her knees and closed her throbbing eyes.

She didn't hear Luke come into the room. He let his gaze linger on her sleek, slender body. He knew every crevice, every secret place. She was so beautiful, she took his breath away.

"Buster, I hate your owner," Sassy mumbled.

Luke snapped off the radio. "Still talking to animals?"

Sassy's head spun around. She let out a gasp. Snatching up the washcloth, she modestly tried to cover herself. "I locked the door."

"You locked one door," he corrected. Rolling up his sleeves, he sat down on the edge of the tub. He nodded toward the door leading to his bedroom. "I came through the other one." He scooped up the sponge bobbing on the water's surface and drew it down her spine.

"Clever," she said. "Well, you can just go out the way you came."

He couldn't suppress a grin. The washcloth was a poor choice of camouflage. He dripped a line of water between her breasts. "It's a little late for that, isn't it? You coming out, or shall I get in?"

She would not be his plaything. "Is that part of the hospitality here? The owner gets to take what he wants?"

His fingers curled around her neck. He fought the urge to tell her he loved her and to beg her to stay. "As I recall the owner got to take what he was offered."

She slapped his hand away. She felt defenseless. "Dammit, get out. A gentleman wouldn't remind a lady she was stupid."

He slid his thumb behind her ear, then lowered his head to press his lips to the sensitive spot. She moved to get out of his reach.

"Sassy, don't you think it's about time you stopped spouting off like a child? If you weren't such a spit-fire, you'd realize the only reason I didn't want you on Sinbad was because I was terrified you might hurt yourself again."

She eyed him warily. "You made that abundantly clear. In front of witnesses no less. When I pick up my Academy Award, I'll be sure to thank you."

He cursed. "I suppose I had that coming."

The circles Luke drew on her back went a notch lower. Sassy released her breath on another gasp. "Were you really terrified for me, or terrified I wouldn't leave on time?"

Luke answered her question with a kiss. Her lips parted. He took and took from her until she went limp. When he let her breathe again, they were both wet. "What do you think?"

"That doesn't excuse your behavior," she said, referring to the kiss that had heated her blood several degrees above the temperature of the water.

"I like the way you smell," he murmured. His tongue traced the lobe of her ear.

She shivered. "You're very good at that."

He loosened the barrettes, then buried his face in her hair. "Your hair is spun gold," he said, kissing her neck. "What am I good at?"

She was beginning to melt. "Changing the subject. You were awful to me in front of everybody. I can't figure you out. You agree with my mother and let her go ahead and plan to turn this place into a circus. Then you tell me I'd better stay healthy so I can leave. You're great at sending mixed signals."

"I'm sorry. I had my reasons."

"Maybe for you. Not for me." Striving to maintain her dignity, Sassy stood up, letting the water drip all over Luke as she stepped over the edge of the tub. With slow deliberate motions, she wrapped the terry-cloth towel around her as if it were a royal cloak. "You don't have to worry about my meeting unscrupulous characters in Hollywood. I've met the master."

He'd come into the room to give her a piece of his mind for defying him. One look at her had stopped him dead. No woman had ever made him furious one minute and want to tumble onto the bed with her the next.

Sassy sat down at the vanity table, lifted her hairbrush, and began to pull it through her hair in long strokes. Static electricity sent a shower of sparkling golden threads around her shoulders. Their gazes met in the mirror. "Luke, unless you came in here to apologize, I suggest you leave." She finished uttering her command and winced.

Luke caught the involuntary movement. Whether she knew it or not, he was responsible for most of her discomfort. His need for her was ferocious, and he wasn't happy about it. He was enough of a realist to know she was simply infatuated with him because he was her first lover. Thinking that she may have other lovers made his skin crawl. He was also realistic enough to know that what he felt for her was more than infatuation—and it was difficult to deal with.

"You've been doing too much," he said. "Chester and I will be back day after tomorrow."

He'd slipped in the information about his leaving so casually, Sassy almost missed it—almost, but not quite. Taken aback, she waited a moment. "Why didn't you tell me you were going away?"

"I just did. I took today off."

"For your pleasure?" she asked, feeling awful.

He could've strangled her. Her eyes darkened with passion, but it was the passion of anger, not need. He waited until he was in control. "For your pleasure as well as mine, I hope."

Sassy choked back a stinging retort. She knew she was thinking more like a spoiled child than a mature woman. And that was the trouble. Thanks to Luke, she now felt like a woman. A rejected woman.

Love, she discovered, hurt. Especially since she hadn't psyched herself up for his imminent departure, and more especially since he hadn't mentioned one word about love to her.

It was ironic. In front of a camera she presented herself as the epitome of cool sophistication and glamour. She knew all the right people and all the right things to say.

Except now. Was this how her mother had felt when her father had left? Unhappy but putting up a good front?

Luke stared at her stiff posture and guessed the problem. He wanted to turn her around and shake her. And he wanted to take off her robe and kiss her until she moaned with desire. Did she think he wasn't hurting too?

He kissed her quickly, before she could protest. She felt his breath whisper through her like a butterfly. She longed to tell him to stay, to ride out in the morning. She wanted him, wanted him to hold her through the night. She wanted to awaken in his arms and let their kiss be the first thing that started the day.

Her hair smelled of soap and perfume, but it was the scent of wildflowers that made him release her. He could lose himself too quickly. "I've got to pack. I'm leaving tonight," he said quietly. If he didn't, he knew he never would.

An eagle flew across the night sky, majestically silhouetted against the moon. Chester and Luke tracked it as it disappeared into the darkness. The embers of the campfire had sputtered and died. Coffee dregs from the bottom of the enamel pot had been scattered on the ground. The only light came from the glowing tip of Chester's cigar and from the stars and the moon. Both men lay on their bedrolls, their heads propped up on their saddles. Nearby the horses nickered softly. Off in the distance they heard the mournful sounds of coyotes.

Luke hadn't told Sassy he was heading for an abandoned gold mine to meet officials from a mining company who'd be flying over by helicopter from Reno at the break of day. If the assay showed the water table wasn't a problem, and if there was enough gold to reopen the mine considering present mining costs, his Circle C Ranch would get a financial shot in the arm. They were big if's, however.

Chester puffed on his cigar. He flicked an ash off the tip. The smoke, less pungent in the night wind, spiraled upward. "I'm getting too old to be sleeping on cold, hard ground. We both know you ran away tonight. And we both know that soon Sassy will be off to La La Land. Then you can tell yourself you were too late. I wasn't proud of you before. You hurt that girl's pride. Fact is, you stepped on her heart."

Luke would have decked any other man who had the nerve to be so blunt. "It won't work."

Chester pushed as only a friend worrying about another could. "Why not?"

Luke's answer was slow in coming, but when it did, it carried conviction. "There's a million reasons why Sassy and I shouldn't be in love, and two million more reasons why we shouldn't get married."

Chester blew a circle of smoke. "I'd say you were past one. What's the other?"

Luke felt each separate muscle in his chest tighten. He'd bungled it badly. He purposely left to give Sassy the space he thought she needed. If it were up to him, he'd have been in bed now with her curled up tight against him, purring.

"Her work and this ranch. They don't mix."

"Baloney," Chester said with a snort. "Then how

come you're letting a bunch of strangers descend on us like locusts? If that's not to keep Sassy here, I don't know what is. Better get your act together, son."

Luke pulled his hat over his face. He didn't mention wanting to meet Sassy's mother. "You're forgetting, old friend, that I've got the experience to know what I'm talking about. It's culture shock to bring a woman like Sassy out here permanently. Besides, I never trust a man who's too stupid to marry the woman he loves but is free with advice."

"What's that supposed to mean?" Chester asked.

"It means, you old goat, that one of these days another man is going to steal Maria away from you. You've been taking her for granted for too long."

Chester snorted but said nothing, which pleased Luke. Admitting to himself he was in love with Sassy was about all he could take for one night.

The next morning, after Sassy and Maria had done their morning chores, Sassy decided to keep her mind off Luke by immersing herself in sketching. She showed Maria the completed book of designs she'd packed in her suitcase.

"These are really terrific designs." Maria's portable sewing machine was set up on a table on the porch. She had used it to mend Sassy's torn jeans.

"This sheath would look marvelous in a liquid lamé." Maria pointed to a sketch of a cocktail dress. "What did you have in mind for this one?"

"I call it Hot Nights. The dress is all black sequins."

Maria offered a suggestion for a white faille dress. "You could use washed denim for this and make it a great daytime outfit. Same design, lower costs, greater profit."

"Maria, that's exactly what I'd been thinking. How do you know all this?"

"Didn't Luke tell you? Sewing is my first love. When my career hit a slump, I considered applying for work at the studio's costume department. But," she added shyly, "I had a personal reason for wanting to come here."

Sassy squeezed her hand. "Chester. I saw how you looked at him yesterday."

Maria smiled. "That's because you're in love with Luke. You know that there's a certain glow."

Blushing, she remembered the first time he'd made love to her. "It shows?"

Maria nodded. "It shows. On Luke too."

Sassy let out a short derisive laugh. "Luke's a confirmed bachelor."

Maria's expression was serious. "Sassy, you've got to understand what Luke's been through. He spent months in rehabilitation, relearning the most ordinary tasks. He used to lie in the hospital and plan like an excited kid. More than anything in the world he wants his own family. We didn't have the heart to tell Luke his intended was a selfish bitch. We knew he needed that drive to get better. When he bought this place, Chester and I watched from the sidelines as Luke poured his heart and soul into making it succeed. He's seen a lot of dreams squashed."

Sassy's stomach churned. Luke still pined for another woman. "He loved her that much?"

"Love, nothing. Cynthia hit that boy when he was down, then she kicked him for good measure. The only thing she accomplished was to make him marriage-shy. Trust, my dear, takes time. I'm sure Luke's afraid to admit his feelings even to himself. He knows you have a whole new career ahead of you. He's sure you'll be a big star. He'd never do anything to stand in your way."

"So I've noticed," Sassy said bitterly. It had been only a day since Luke had last touched her, since she'd let herself be lost in the emotions only he could evoke. If it were this difficult to be separated from him for a short time, what would it be like to be separated for weeks or months?

"And what about your career?" Maria asked gently.

"I'm more than ready to move on into fashion designing. True, I may be young, but thanks to the years I've spent as a model, I know what women my age are interested in buying. It makes perfect sense to me that I can design clothes anywhere. I'm not looking to form a giant corporation. If I can interest a design house in some sort of deal, that's fine."

Maria snapped the locks on the top of her sewing machine case.

"Sassy, if you love Luke enough, you'll fight for him. It happens that I know four excellent seamstresses in town who'd jump at the chance to earn extra money. We could have your samples sewn in a few days with all of us working. The rest is up to you."

Sassy's eyes flashed with hope and determination.

"You're absolutely right. Where would I get the materials I need?"

Maria picked up the sewing machine and headed for the screen door. "Las Vegas," she said simply. Maria waited while Sassy opened the door to let her through. "A friend of mine owns a firm that makes costumes for the hotels. She stocks most kinds of materials."

Maria made a series of phone calls, first to her friend in Las Vegas, then to her four seamstress friends. They all agreed to help.

In Vegas Sassy bought what she needed to begin her sample collection. By evening they were back at the ranch, tired yet exhilarated. The picnic tables in the kitchen were cleared off to be used for cutting the muslin patterns. With Sassy and Maria sharing their innermost feelings, and with each respecting the talent of the other, their friendship moved to a new plane. Before turning in for the night, they sat sipping lemonade.

"Sassy, where will you show your first collection?"

She put down the swatch of black wool crepe. "It depends. We need press coverage, so it's got to be a convenient place for the buyers to attend. New York City would be ideal for a showroom, since it's the heart of the garment industry. We can ship the clothes we make here to wherever we need to."

She still had to break the news to her mother. She realized that Peter and Beth were right. Her mother was still a young woman with a fine reputation. She'd put out the word to help get her other clients. That night before falling asleep Sassy drew up a tentative list.

Maria's seamstress friends showed up at the dot of nine the next day eager to begin. Patterns, fit to Sassy's measurements, were cut out of the muslin then transferred to the materials brought back from Vegas. The women understood exactly what Sassy wanted. Soon the hum of portable sewing machines filled the air. Maria, with her nimble, talented fingers, did the detail work.

Sassy brewed coffee, drank more than was good for her, baked an apple pie, and paced nervously.

"Sit down, you're driving us crazy." Maria said. She snipped a thread from the first completed dress. "Here you are."

Hot Nights was a shimmering work of art brought to fruition because of Maria. Tears of gratitude filled Sassy's eyes. "I can't believe it. My dream's come true. Our first dress under the SASSY label. Thank you. Thank you all." None of the women missed the generous way she included them in her happiness.

Sassy slipped into the garment immediately. It fit like a second skin. She pirouetted for them, and they all hugged one another. "We're not running a sweatshop here, ladies. Maria, you know you're dying to go home with Margaret. Go. I'll see you tomorrow." Over Maria's faint objections, Sassy shooed her out the door. With their promises to return the next morning, Sassy bid the women good night.

Sassy flew into her bedroom on winged feet. She studied herself in the full-length mirror. Lowering her lids, she thrust her hips forward, adopting a sexy stance. Then in a fit of joy, her eyes glowing with happiness, she tossed her head, letting her hair fly around her face. The low-cut strapless neckline trembled as she fought to steady her breath. Laughing, she unzipped the dress, stepping out of it carefully.

"Not bad." In fact, Luke thought she looked terrific. Happy to be back, he leaned against the doorjamb thoroughly enjoying the view of Sassy in her strapless black teddy cut high at the thighs. She gasped at his presence. Wariness and pleasure—he saw both in her eyes. "I missed you, Sassy. Looks like things have changed around here. Whose mannequin did I trip over?"

She quickly hung up her dress. "A friend of Maria's. Do you mind?" Could he hear her heart rattling around in her chest? She was afraid to make mistakes, afraid to be the baby Luke had called her the night she'd asked him to make love to her. Then it had been a tender endearment, whispered on her lips before he'd spun her into the stratosphere. Now she was a woman in every sense of the word. She would fight for the man she loved.

Luke lifted a brow. He'd missed her terribly. He didn't know which was worse—dreaming about her while he knew she occupied his bed, or the thought of dreaming about her after she had left him. He'd done a lot of thinking on that hard, cold ground after Chester had chewed him out, a lot of planning which had included her. "What's going on?"

Sassy sat down on the bed and told him. Simply, without the fanfare and sense of excitement that was bubbling inside her. As was her style, she praised Maria and the others for making her sample collection possible.

Her eyes shone with delight. "We want it to be ready to be previewed when Jamie Rudolpho arrives."

Luke hooked his hands in his pockets and rocked back on his heels. There was a quiet energy about her. And there was something else too. A measure of assurance in her ability to succeed on her own in a new venture. He wondered how her mother would accept the changes in her daughter.

"Seems to me you've started a cottage industry under my nose. Sassy, the dress is wonderful. I've never seen you look lovelier." He took her hands, drawing her to him. "No, that's not true. I like you better naked and under me."

Her nerves tingled. Luke's eyes were dark, darker than she'd ever seen them. His long hair curled at the edge of his collar. The top and sides were wind-blown. He needed a shave. And he was the most desirable man she'd ever seen. She caught his scent and breathed in deeply. "How was your business meeting?"

"Fine." Her eyes were bluer today, he thought, her skin softer. The scent of wildflowers drifted from her. He wasn't interested in talking business or dwelling on how well it had gone. The gold mine would reopen in a month. All he had wanted to do was race back home. Incredibly, he'd begun to think about the place as a home not a house. "It went well. I've leased a parcel of land to a mining company. And I'm going to build a separate house for Maria. It's time those cowpunchers ate somewhere else." He hoped Sassy understood the significance of his words.

He cupped her face in his hands, gazing at her in silence. He had to assure himself she still wanted him. With an urgency akin to desperation, his mouth covered hers. He could feel the pounding of her heart as passion ignited passion. But when his hands lowered to press her closer, she twisted away.

"No." She pushed at his chest, her chest heaving with emotion. "I can't let you do this to me, not until I've said my piece. Sit down, Luke. I've got a lot to say." Wrapping a bathrobe around her, she gave herself the distance she needed. Pacing the floor, she began. "In the first place, I will not be a convenient receptacle for your pleasure."

At her unexpected choice of words, he cursed vividly. "I didn't ride five hours for a convenient receptacle as you so crudely put it. I'm not that hard up."

She stared into his hard eyes for a moment. Maria's advice came storming into her mind. "In the second place, I know you've been hurt in the past, but that's no reason for you to think all women are like Cynthia."

His jaw clenched. "I never said they were."

"No, but you act that way. Luke, please be quiet until I'm through. You're making me nervous." She took a deep breath. "I think it's only fair to tell you that I'm in love with you." She held up her hands as

Luke's mouth opened. "No, don't you dare say anything. I've decided to lay my cards on the table. If I had more time, which thanks to my mother and you, I don't, I wouldn't be saying this. I'd make you fall in love with me and have you think it was all your idea. Keep quiet, Luke Cassidy."

Luke squelched the desire to take Sassy in his arms. She was magnificent—fire and femininity, passion and purity.

"In the third place," Sassy continued, her eyes bright with tears, "no woman could love you more than I do. I've had years to dream of my own family and what I want from life. I'm sorry if you don't like hearing this, but after I saw you help the cow give birth to her calf, that clinched it. I knew I wanted you for my husband."

Luke's brows rose in disbelief. He couldn't contain himself any longer. He ached for her, yet he was amused. His mustache twitched uncontrollably. "That's hardly the most flattering remark I've ever heard, Sassy. Most men don't want to be romantically compared to cattle."

"Be quiet," she said, knowing she was botching things, yet unable to restrain herself. "This is real life, Luke, not some fairytale, not some story where the man knocks over all his opposition until the girl comes to her senses."

"Forgive me," he murmured. Joy soared in his heart. Later Sassy would know just exactly how he intended to knock over all his opposition.

She lifted her shoulders. "I saw how kind you were to an animal in distress, and the cowboys had already told me how good you are to them, to say nothing of Chester and Maria. I knew, like it or not, Luke, that you were a nice man. You're not as nice as I hoped, because you won't let me ride Sinbad again," she said with a smile, "but that's minor. I intend to do it anyway, so we're even. You've got a good heart, even if it's buried behind cynicism. You're wonderfully handsome, although I'd probably love you if you didn't have a strand of hair. You'll father beautiful children. Whether you know it or not, you have romantic qualities. This room is a fine example. On the other hand, I think you should know that stubbornness is my major fault . . ." Her voice trailed off. She seemed to be wondering if there were any points she'd missed.

He grinned, itching to kiss the serious look off her face. "I never noticed."

She paced to the window. "You're afraid no woman would want to live here away from everything. Well, that's stupid. There're planes, trains, cars, buses, even pickup trucks that connect you to the rest of the world. I can't think of a better place for children to grow up. I warn you I want a lot of them. It's not fashionable nowadays, but I don't care. I've already looked up the population of Humboldt County. Even with the people of Winnemucca making up forty percent of the population, there's only 1.3 people per square mile, so it can stand a few more. I love you, you big lug, and I'm the best thing that ever happened to you. If you let me get away, you'll regret it. Anyway, I've decided honesty is the best policy." Sniffling, she reached for a tissue.

Luke slowly advanced toward her. Tenderly, he wiped away her tears. Very deliberately he put his finger on her lips, stilling the wonderful jumble of words that threatened to spill forth. He brushed his hand through her glorious array of hair.

"Sassy, darling, shut up. You're ranting. In the first place, you precious little witch, I know you're the best thing that's ever happened to me. I've known it far longer than you can imagine. Since you stepped off the plane. In the second place, I have a few wants too. They all start and end with you. I want to see your name inscribed in the family Bible. We'll have to use your real name, Serena. Heaven forbid that our great, great, grandchildren know their gorgeous ancestor, who could have been a famous movie star, gave me such a hard time when I rode hell-bent-for-leather to ask her to marry me."

Sassy looked dumbfounded. "You did?"

"Definitely." He kissed her forehead.

"Then why," she said softly, "did you let me go on?"

He chuckled. "As I recall, you told me to be quiet each time I opened my mouth. Of course, now that you've shown me this pushy side of your character, I might change my mind and take back my proposal."

Leaping into his arms, she flung hers around his neck. She kissed his cheeks, his eyes, his mouth. "Try it and you'll never get out of here alive, cowboy."

He swept her up, he carried her to the bed. "A real boss."

With a moan, she brought his lips to hers, while her fingers found the buttons on his shirt. Only when flesh met flesh did her body tremble with satisfaction.

"This is how I dreamed of you last night," Luke said with a groan, stroking the woman he worshiped. He would have sworn the flowers on the sheets had bloomed. The room was hers now, no other woman had or would ever live in it with him.

"Oh, Luke," Sassy said on a sigh, guiding him to her, "I love you."

"And I you."

Long after she fell asleep, Luke lay awake. Unless Mrs. Shaw blessed their union, Sassy's happiness wouldn't be complete.

Eleven

Jamie Rudolpho, along with his photographer, hairstylist, and lighting and makeup crew arrived the day Sassy's collection was ready. Thin and wiry with sparse brown hair, the man who had been born John Rudolph gave the impression of being in motion even when he was standing still. His blue eyes traveled over the desert country chosen for the location of his shoot.

"This is marvelous." He pumped Luke's hand. "Sassy, your mother's picked a winner." Neither Sassy nor Luke bothered to tell him her mother had never seen the ranch or that Sassy's nervousness stemmed from the showdown that was sure to happen when her mother arrived. "Luke, where are the horses? I imagine you use quarter horses here." Seeing the fields of grain, he said, "I see you grow your own feed. Very sensible."

The man's enthusiasm for horses caught Luke by surprise. In faded jeans and cowboy boots that looked as if they'd seen a good workout, the man was nothing like Luke had expected him to be. With a laugh of appreciation he realized Jamie Rudolpho was a frustrated cowboy. Chuckling, he led the fashion designer over to the corral, where Sinbad, saddled and ready, snorted at the newcomer.

"This is Sinbad. He's already got the star syndrome."

Jamie eyed the horse. "Think I could ride him?"

"Do you know how?"

Jamie grinned. "Is water wet?" Swinging open the gate, he spoke softly to the horse, stroking his flank. With the agility of a man born to ride bareback, Jamie swung a leg over, lifting himself into the creaking saddle. And with a dramatic flourish of his hand, he picked up the reins. "See ya!" Horse and rider galloped off. Luke and Sassy lost them in a cloud of dust.

Luke laughed. "Well, what do you know?"

Jamie returned whooping with joy about twenty minutes later. He'd earned Luke's and everyone else's respect and a host of new male friends. Luke also knew he'd take direction from this man.

Jamie brushed trail dust from his trousers. His eyes shone with happiness. "I'd give half my fortune to be able to design my collection from here. Lord, look at all this space. Do you realize there's no one between you and the sky? Makes a man feel invincible."

"Where are you from, Jamie?" Luke handed him a cold beer. Jamie wiped his forehead with a handkerchief.

"Hell's Kitchen in New York—not the nicest neighborhood. We played with guns and knives. With my interest in fashion, I played with a lot more guns than I'd have liked. When I was a kid, I got to go away to camp for two weeks. It was sponsored by the Fresh Air Fund. That's an organization to help underprivileged kids. There was a Shetland pony at the camp. By the time I went home, I had graduated to riding a full-size horse. I was hooked. Besides designing, it's the only thing I have time for. You're lucky, Luke. Real lucky."

Luke knew he was lucky for more reasons than that. Still he worried about Sassy. "You're welcome anytime, Jamie. Isn't that right, honey?" His hand slid possessively around Sassy's waist.

The action declared his intentions. Maria and Chester exchanged approving glances.

Jamie took a long swig of beer. Sassy's face was flushed with pleasure. "Does your mother know?"

"She will," Luke said, answering for her. "She'll be arriving the last day of the shoot, along with the brass from the Jenson and Dooley advertising agency."

Jamie refused a second beer, opting for a soda instead. "As an interested designer, whose clothes are you wearing? I warn you I can be the jealous type."

Sassy's mint-green bolero jacket fit strikingly over plum-colored slacks and matching blouse. "You're the first person in the trade to see a SASSY original." She grinned, her turquoise eyes filled with delight. "I need your advice."

Jamie jumped up. He threw his head back and laughed. "That's wonderful! You've finally done it. Luke, this kid and I go back twenty years. She hounded me incessantly, borrowing paper and pencils, sketching her little hands to the bone whenever she was made to wait."

Grabbing her hands, he insisted she show him the rest of the line. "Tomorrow, young lady, you work for me. Today I can still be your friend and offer advice. There's more to running a business than making lines on paper. Ask your mother. She'll tell you."

His comment, reminding her that her mother was very much responsible for her good fortune, doused a good deal of Sassy's giddiness. Luke smiled at her. "It'll all work out," he said, adding when they were alone how much he loved her.

Maria, her jet-black hair coiled in thick braids around her head, wore another of Sassy's creations. It was she who'd insisted each of them wear one of Sassy's outfits. "Nothing like walking advertisements."

The magenta denim split skirt had a matching overblouse. Looped casually with a gold interlocking belt worn low, the outfit was accentuated by Maria's coloring.

Jamie's sharp eyes appreciatively observed Maria, who was serving a platter of sandwiches to the hungry crew. Chester stood by, his face set in an inscrutable mask.

Maria swept by.

"Who is she?" Jamie asked, his gaze never leaving Maria. "She's got the most extraordinary face I've ever seen."

Sassy caught Chester's bleak expression and smiled to herself. She held out her hand. "Maria, come meet Jamie Rudolpho."

"Maria, maybe we can get together later and you can show me Sassy's other creations. Sassy," Jamie said meaningfully, "I'm sure you and Luke won't mind." Jamie's reputation as a fast worker drew a raised brow from Luke.

Maria glanced at Sassy, who subtly nodded toward Chester. "I'll be glad to show them to you."

Jamie pushed his sunglasses back on his head. He rose to take Maria's hand. "This may sound like a line, Maria, but haven't I seen you before?"

"You might have seen her in the movies," Luke added. Chester moved away from the wall. Luke gripped Sassy's wrist in time for her to see Chester scowling.

"Maria, can I see you a minute?" Chester locked her upper arm, dragging her away before she could answer Jamie.

"Did I miss something here?" Jamie asked.

Luke slapped the man's shoulder. "Unless I miss my guess, you've just accomplished what Maria and I haven't been able to do in years."

Jamie shrugged his shoulders, accepting defeat. "Yeah. He did look as though he wanted to kill me. Shall I keep it up until there's a ring on her finger?"

"Yes," Luke and Sassy chimed in unison. The three went indoors, where Sassy showed Jamie the other sample clothes. Luke observed her troubled expression when Jamie once again brought her mother's name into the conversation.

"I always thought she worked you too hard. Sassy, after this is over, let's sit down and really talk business. We may be able to work out an arrangement."

"I'd like nothing better," Sassy assured him.

Her work began at five A.M. Sassy arose, leaving Luke still asleep in their warm bed as she made her way into the bathroom shivering.

She washed and dressed, then started to tiptoe past Luke toward the door. Luke waited for her to pass him. He snaked out his hand to capture her arm. "Come here."

"Shhhh. I didn't mean to wake you. Go back to sleep."

"Not without a kiss." She went willingly. "Mmmm, nice. How many names do you want in the family Bible?"

Her breath caught in her throat. "You ask me that now, and expect me to leave you?"

He caught her face in his hands. "I want you to think about that today. Tonight, you can give me your answer. I love you, funny face. Think about me when they're trying to make you beautiful."

She brushed her lips over his, then lingered to taste him more thoroughly. Would she ever get tired of hearing him tease her? The fact that Luke wanted children thrilled her. Thanksgiving, she thought happily, would be a family affair. Her only wish was that her mother be with them. "I love you, too, cowboy, but if you don't let me go, we'll have a crowd in here before you know it."

His hand fondled her breast. "Did I ever tell you that when this is over and you're back from California, you and I are going to hide out for a month? I'm very anxious to see our first child's name in that Bible."

Sassy worked tirelessly from sunup to sundown. By the end of the first day's shooting, not one of the cowpunchers hanging close to the ranch thought a model's life was easy. When she tumbled into bed that night after a long, hot bath, Luke gave her one of his magical liniment rubs, then held her in his arms while she fell into a deep sleep.

Sassy sat on a stool in one of the campers the crew had come in, talking to the hairstylist while her hair was combed, sprayed, and arranged around her face.

The photographer, Mike Kincaid, had ordered the windblown look for the morning. "One of these days, Sassy, we ought to bottle your beauty," the stylist said.

"My sentiments exactly. But I'll keep the original." Luke ducked his head through the door. He wore chaps over his jeans. His plaid shirt was rolled up to show off his muscled arms. A hat hung down his back. He gave her hand a quick squeeze. "Honey, do you think you'll be able to smile while I sweep you off your feet? We're going to be riding pretty fast. Mike wants your hair flowing in the wind. Since there is none, we'll have to churn it up by using speed." Luke leaned over to whisper in her ear. Sassy's face flamed. Her eyes glowed. "I've had plenty of practice galloping at breakneck speed with you, haven't I?"

The photographer got the shot he wanted on the first take. For the rest of the day, Sassy and Luke worked at another area of the ranch. Phyllis Shaw, arriving days earlier than expected, was waiting by Jamie's side when Luke reined in the horse.

The older woman beamed as Luke helped Sassy down from Sinbad. "Darling, that was marvelous. Let me see you." She held Sassy at arm's length. "The mountains and the air must agree with you. I've never seen you look more beautiful."

Luke waited by Sassy's side. He handed Sinbad's reins to Junior, who would cool down and feed the horse.

"Mother, this is Luke Cassidy. Luke, my mother, Phyllis Shaw."

Phyllis Shaw glanced from one to the other, her eyes narrowing. The current flowing between the two young people was unmistakable. So that's the lay of the land, she said to herself.

"A pleasure to meet you, Luke. Thanks for taking care of my daughter. By this time next year you can brag that you've taken care of a star." The silence told her what she wanted to know. The quicker she got Sassy away from this man, the better.

Sassy tucked her arm in her mother's. "Let's go inside. We can catch up on gossip." She made the introductions as she steered her mother to her room. "I have some news to tell you," she said, as soon as her mother was seated.

Phyllis Shaw patted her daughter's hand. She looked prim and neat in a white linen suit. "It'll keep. I have some news to tell you first. You've already been offered a second movie contract. Isn't that marvelous, darling? I worked so hard to get it for you."

Sassy pushed the guilt aside. She'd heard her mother use the same methods before to keep her in line. "You should have asked me first. I don't want it."

"Are you crazy?" Phyllis Shaw charged off her seat. "Have you totally lost your mind? Who turns down a chance of a lifetime?"

Her mother's words gave Sassy the opening she needed. She picked up her mother's hand. "No smart person turns down the chance of a lifetime. That's why I'm declining the second movie. I simply have no interest in being before the camera any longer." She clutched her mother's fingers. "I'm in love with Luke."

"With a cowboy?" Phyllis Shaw's eyebrows rose along with her voice.

"With a man," Sassy corrected. "Please, mother, I love you both, but Luke is the man I'm going to spend my life with."

"Bring him in here," her mother ordered.

Luke's arm was around Sassy's shoulders when they returned. Sassy, pale and shaken, stood tall and proud. Her eyes welled up with tears.

"This is all your doing, young man. I should have known that was the reason you agreed to have Rudolpho's layout shot here."

Luke had promised himself to treat her with respect. "Mrs. Shaw, I'm not denying I had a reason. Knowing how little time Sassy and I had, I would have done anything to keep her here, short of blackmail. Please consider carefully what you're doing. Sassy told me how you kept her father's desertion from her and the pain it caused. Doesn't she deserve to make her own decisions about her future? I know you love her, but I wonder if you love her as much as I do. You see, without your blessing, I won't marry her." At Sassy's sudden gasp, he turned to her. His expression softened automatically.

"Darling, your mother is your only family. I don't want to come between you. Not having your father as part of your life was cruel, but there's nothing anyone can do about it. Remember when you told me that your mother gave you Christmas presents from him? As far as I'm concerned, your father lost out on seeing the most wonderful daughter in the world grow up to be a lovely woman. More than anything in the world, I want to marry you and have children with you. But I can't add to the cruelty you've already suffered. In time you'd resent me if our children's grandmother wouldn't come and visit."

"Luke, don't do this," whispered a broken-hearted Sassy. She saw their dreams crumbling before her eyes. "Why, Luke? I love you. Don't do this to us."

He had taken a gamble with their future without telling her. It was up to him to convince her mother he was right, for all their sakes. "Darling, it's the only way. Trust me." He lifted a hand to brush away a tear.

"Mrs. Shaw, I love Sassy so much I want her happiness over my own. Enough so that I wouldn't stand in her way no matter what career she chose or where she wanted to live. Can you say the same thing? Do you love her that much?"

Phyllis Shaw said nothing. She seemed to be reliving a moment from long ago. "Is this what you truly want, Sassy?"

"More than anything in the world. Even before I fell in love with Luke, I was trying to find a way to let you know I wanted to follow my own path."

Phyllis Shaw was not about to lose her daughter the way she'd lost her husband. The loneliness would be unbearable. She gazed from one to the other.

Sighing, she spoke to Luke. A small smile formed on her lips. Maybe all wasn't lost. "I can see why my daughter fell in love with you. Luke Cassidy, you're a first rate bastard. You've used the only argument on me that could possibly work."

The tension flowed from Luke's shoulders. "What's that?"

"I've known for some time that Sassy wasn't thrilled with modeling. She never wanted to do the movie. Fashion designing has always been her interest. It was inevitable. So I've accepted a few other clients. I was going to tell you about it, Sassy."

Sassy went along with the pretense. It was her mother's way of releasing her with her blessings. "Mother, I'm so glad." Sassy threw her arms around the older woman.

Luke smiled. He could afford to be generous to his soon-to-be mother-in-law. "What was the argument, Mrs. Shaw?"

She thrust out her hand. "Phyllis. As long as we're going to be related, you might as well call me Phyllis."

"The argument, mother?" Sassy kept her mother close.

"Perhaps if your father ever looked at me with the love in his eyes this man has for you, things would have been different. Who can tell? When Luke said he was willing to give you up for your own happiness, he made me realize how selfish I've been. Maybe if I hadn't insisted on a career for you, we'd still be a family. But, Sassy, there was so much going on with your father and me that I never told you about. Believe me when I say it was my greatest wish to have you two reunited before he died. It wasn't meant to be. But, honey, I only wanted a secure future for you."

"Mother," Sassy said in a choked voice, "I love you." The two women kissed. They were equals now in ways that would only enrich their lives.

Luke looked fondly down at both of them. He put an arm around each. "Ladies, it occurs to me that Sassy will need a representative for her business in New York once she completes her movie. Naturally, this representative will have to keep in close touch with us, visiting often to discuss business. Now, if this representative also happens to be the grandmother of Sassy's and my children, she could kill two birds with one stone, so to speak. There'd be a guest room ready for her whenever she felt the urge to see the kids."

Phyllis Shaw wiped her cheeks. "And if the children happened to be beautiful, and if their parents didn't mind, I could arrange an occasional modeling layout. It would help with the children's college fund. What do you think, Luke?"

Luke gave her a loud kiss. "I think it's great."

"Humph. Well, don't ever expect me to ride a horse when I come. I'll leave that nonsense to my daughter."

Luke hugged Sassy. "Now I know where you got your pushy attitude."

"What is he talking about, Sassy?" Mrs. Shaw asked.

Sassy looked at Luke, giggling. "Nothing you'd be interested in."

Shaking her head, Phyllis Shaw left the two young people alone. Young people needed secrets. She needed a drink, and a quiet place to think about the future.

"Pushy, huh?" Sassy threw her arms around Luke's neck. Then, dragging his face to hers, she said, "Lord, I love you, cowboy. What would you have done if my mother hadn't given us her blessing?"

It took a while for Luke to answer. He was too busy kissing his future wife. He nibbled her bottom lip. "Then I'd have shown both of you what pushy meant."

THE EDITOR'S CORNER

Get ready for a month chockfull of adventure and romance! In October our LOVESWEPT heroes are a bold and dashing group, and you'll envy the heroines who win their hearts.

Starting off the month, we have **HOT TOUCH,** LOVESWEPT #354. Deborah Smith brings to life a dreamy hero in rugged vet Paul Belue. When Caroline Fitzsimmons arrives at Paul's bayou mansion to train his pet wolf for a movie, she wishes she could tame the male of her species the way she works her magic with animals. The elegant and mysterious Caroline fascinates Paul and makes him burn for her caresses, and when he whispers "Chere" in his Cajun drawl, he melts her resistance. A unique and utterly sensual romance, **HOT TOUCH** sizzles!

Your enthusiastic response to Gail Douglas's work has thrilled us all and has set Gail's creative juices flowing. Her next offering is a quartet of books called *The Dreamweavers.* Hop onboard for your first romantic journey with Morgan Sinclair in LOVESWEPT #355, **SWASHBUCKLING LADY.** Morgan and her three sisters run The Dreamweavers, an innovative travel company. And you'll be along for the ride to places exotic as each falls in love with the man of her dreams.

When hero Cole Jameson spots alluring pirate queen Morgan, he thinks he's waltzed into an old Errol Flynn movie! But Morgan enjoys her role as Captain of a restored brigantine, and she plays it brilliantly for the tourists of Key West. In Morgan, Cole finds a woman who's totally guileless, totally without pretense—and he doesn't know how to react to her honesty, especially since he can't disclose his own reasons for being in Key West. Intrigued and infuriated by Cole's elusive nature, Morgan thinks she's sailing in unchar-

(continued)

tered waters. We guarantee you'll love these two charming characters—or we'll walk the plank!

One of our favorite writing teams, Adrienne Staff and Sally Goldenbaum return with **THE GREAT AMERICAN BACHELOR,** LOVESWEPT #356. Imagine you're on the worst blind date of your life . . . and then you're spirited away on a luxury yacht by a handsome hunk known in the tabloids as the Great American Bachelor! Cathy Stevenson is saved—literally—by Michael Winters when he pulls her from the ocean, and her nightmare turns into a romantic dream. Talk about envying a heroine! You'll definitely want to trade places with Cathy in this story of a modern day Robinson Crusoe and his lady love!

Peggy Webb will take you soaring beyond the stars with **HIGHER THAN EAGLES,** LOVESWEPT #357. From the first line you'll be drawn into this powerfully evocative romance.

A widow with a young son, Rachel Windham curses the fates who've brought the irresistible pilot Jacob Donovan back from his dangerous job of fighting oil rig fires. Jacob stalks her relentlessly, demanding she explain why she'd turned her back on him and fled into marriage to another man, and Rachel can't escape—not from the mistakes of the past, nor the yearning his mere presence stirs in her. Peggy does a superb job in leading Rachel and Jacob full circle through their hurts and disappointments to meet their destiny in each other's arms.

Next in our LOVESWEPT lineup is #358, **FAMILIAR WORDS** by Mary Kay McComas. Mary Kay creates vividly real characters in this sensitive love story between two single parents.

Beth Simms is mortified when her little boy, Scotty, calls ruggedly handsome Jack Reardan "daddy" during the middle of Sunday church services. She knows that every male Scotty sees is "daddy," but

(continued)

there's something different about this man whose wicked teasing makes her blush. Jack bulldozes Beth's defenses and forges a path straight to her heart. You won't want to miss this lively tale, it's peppered with humor and emotion as only Mary Kay can mix them!

Barbara Boswell finishes this dazzling month with **ONE STEP FROM PARADISE,** LOVESWEPT #359. Police officer Lianna Novak is furious when she's transferred to Burglary, but desire overwhelms her fury when she meets Detective Michael Kirvaly. Urged on by wild, dangerous feelings for Michael, Lianna risks everything by falling in love with her new partner. Michael's undeniable attraction to Lianna isn't standard operating procedure, but the minute the sultry firecracker with the sparkling eyes approached his desk, he knew he'd never let her go—even if he had to handcuff her to him and throw away the key. Barbara will really capture your heart with this delightful romance.

We're excited and curious to know what you think of our new look, so do write and tell us. We hope you enjoy it!

Best wishes from the entire LOVESWEPT staff,
Sincerely,

Carolyn Nichols

Carolyn Nichols
Editor
LOVESWEPT
Bantam Books
666 Fifth Avenue
New York, NY 10103

60 Minutes to a Better, More Beautiful You!

Now it's easier than ever to awaken your sensuality, stay slim forever—even make yourself irresistible. With Bantam's bestselling subliminal audio tapes, you're only 60 minutes away from a better, more beautiful you!

__	45004-2	**Slim Forever**	$8.95
__	45112-X	**Awaken Your Sensuality**	$7.95
__	45081-6	**You're Irresistible**	$7.95
__	45035-2	**Stop Smoking Forever**	$8.95
__	45130-8	**Develop Your Intuition**	$7.95
__	45022-0	**Positively Change Your Life**	$8.95
__	45154-5	**Get What You Want**	$7.95
__	45041-7	**Stress Free Forever**	$7.95
__	45106-5	**Get a Good Night's Sleep**	$7.95
__	45094-8	**Improve Your Concentration**	$7.95
__	45172-3	**Develop A Perfect Memory**	$8.95

Bantam Books, Dept. LT, 414 East Golf Road, Des Plaines, IL 60016

Please send me the items I have checked above. I am enclosing $_____ (please add $2.00 to cover postage and handling). Send check or money order, no cash or C.O.D.s please. (Tape offer good in USA only.)

Mr/Ms _____

Address _____

City/State _____ Zip_____

LT-8/89

Please allow four to six weeks for delivery. This offer expires 2/90.
Prices and availability subject to change without notice.